ME.... ...

CHRISTMAS

How it might have been.

Chris Prater

Men At Christmas

CONTENTS

Men At Christmas

1. The Priest: Zechariah

The light blinded him. Brighter than the sun, yet he felt no pain. It shattered the dimness of the room where he stood and seemed to blaze all around him. He stood transfixed, adrenalin coursing, fear rising. The emanating rays appeared to blend into lines, the lines coalescing into shapes. He sensed...'presence'; a powerful, strong presence, radiating from the light. He recognised waist, one hand, then another; arms chest and shoulders became clear. He had been alone in that place, yet now...he was not alone. A man stood before him, a man of light, face of gold, like no other he had ever seen. From another world, from another realm of being, the man stood there and he shrank back in terror. Another kingdom had penetrated the one he knew. Despite all his learning, all his knowledge he felt totally unprepared either to meet or to deal with this appearance. Shaken to the core he could hardly stand before the one before him.
Then the man spoke.

***

As she stooped a shadow fell over her. A man stood above her.
"What are you doing here at this time of day?" He said.

Turing around, the old woman felt accused.
"Drawing water for the garden."
"The level is low, this must be the last time."
She knew she had taken a risk and felt the blood
rush to her cheeks in shame.
"If the drought continues we will have to limit
ourselves to drinking only." The village elder was
firm, but respectful also of the old woman. Her
husband had taught him at school. His voice
softened still further as he realised the woman's
sense of shame.
"Please make this the last time Elizabeth."
"The last time. I give you my word."

She was grateful for the honour he had shown her.
Returning up the slope to her garden she dipped a
beaker in the jar and carefully poured the precious
liquid round the base of the plants. The dry soil
drank it eagerly. She went into the house and
returned with stick and seed; still time to plant the
late melons. The patch had been dug that morning,
loosing the earth with the spike and breaking up the
dry clods with the club. Now with the dibbing stick
she formed a hole in the dust dropped in two seeds
poured in a little water and covered them. It had
been a lot of effort yet, as she looked up at the blue
sky, she knew that if heaven didn't send any rain the
seed would die within the soil and there would be
no fruit from all her labour.

Men At Christmas

Four Weeks Earlier

***

Zechariah moved aside a lock of grey hair and kissed Elizabeth's forehead. Their eyes met again and again they turned aside from that look of intimacy.

Strange, that after so long, they had not become accustomed to it. But with the years, rather than weaken, the inability to gaze into each other's eyes had intensified, for, looking deeply into her eyes, seemed only to bring to the surface that emptiness in their lives which, still, neither of them could face.

"How long will you be gone?" Her question was empty for she already knew the answer.

"Just over the month." He replied gently but still looking away.

"I'm sorry not to be going with you this time." This was said with more ease for it was true. She had often gone up with him but this year the lack of rain made watering the garden essential. One month more like this and their vegetables would have withered into the parched soil and their fruit would have fallen prematurely from the vine and trees. They needed their harvest for there was lack enough already.

"I understand," he said but it would not be easy for either of them. These days he found the noisy city such a challenge after the peace of his village and garden; he would have liked Elizabeth's company.

He took his bag and stick, stroked aside the grey lock that had fallen over her forehead again, kissed her and walked slowly from the house. She accompanied him to the edge of the garden and saw him walk up the slope to join the two friends who were making the journey with him.

Elizabeth worked hard in the garden that morning until the sun climbed towards mid heaven. Then she rested indoors in the noon day heat. She was thankful she still had a healthy body. Judith, whom she would visit this evening, was her age and had been bedridden these last five months. She could still talk, oh how she could talk, much more so than Elizabeth, but old age had robbed her of strength in her limbs and she was dependent upon others visiting her now.

With Zechariah gone, Elizabeth thought again of their life together.

Their marriage had been arranged of course but she had been glad it had been to Zechariah. No priestly match had been found for one of her sisters and a man outside of the Aaronic line had had to be found instead. It had upset her father she knew. But for Elizabeth herself, a daughter of Aaron, a young priest from the division of Abijah had been found and on the supreme day of her life she joined him beneath the huppah and felt fortunate. They were young, ambitious, had both received a right match and had high hopes of serving God together in the priestly line. Zechariah, she had heard, was meticulous and took his duties very seriously. He attended carefully to his studies and teaching, and ensured that they both lived by the Law. She knew and admired his heart of devotion and walked with him knowing fully that his standing before God and in the community was also her own.

They had known a real appreciation for each other. They enjoyed each other's companionship and love blossomed in those early days. They had rejoiced in each other's arms and delighted in the other's embrace. As the months turned into years, though, a problem seemed to force itself upon their marriage. At first they joined happily in the ceremonies surrounding the births of the children of their friends and peers, later it became harder to do so for, as the years passed by, they had no such ceremony to invite others to share. They met in love, but there appeared to be no essential meeting; there was no result from their union. Like seed upon rocky ground their love seemed unable to penetrate into fruitfulness and a wedge was relentlessly driven between them. Elizabeth never forgot that day when in desperation she had clung to Zechariah's robe and sobbed, 'Give me children or I die!' He had long been ready with Jacob's answer to Rachel; 'Am I in the place of God who has kept you from having children!' The words had stung her to her heart and even to this day gave pain at the remembrance of them.

In those years Elizabeth, particularly, had drawn strength from the scriptures. God had opened Rachel's womb and she had given birth to two fine sons Joseph and Benjamin; one the saviour of his people in famine, the other the founder of a major tribe in Israel. But it was Hannah especially who was Elizabeth's heroine. Not only had Hannah been barren but her husband's other, fruitful, wife made her life so unbearable that finally she cried out to God vowing that if He gave her a son she in turn would give him back to the Lord. And so Samuel had been born, the great, last judge of Israel who had anointed both Saul and David as kings. God could not be out given though and Hannah had gone on to have three more sons and two daughters.

Elizabeth longed to bear even one such son. There had been that unforgettable journey to Jerusalem for Passover when in great anguish she had stood in the temple courts and vowed that if God would give her a son she would dedicate him to the Lord to serve him not merely as a priest but as an exemplary, righteous priest. Like Hannah, Elizabeth had wept there at the holy place. Unlike Hannah though, there was no answer; the heavens seemed as hard as brass, her womb as barren as the wasteland. The years ground on until that time came when the way it was with women was no

longer the way it was with her and she wept and
wept again over the utter frustration, the broken
dreams and the hardness of her lot. It was then that
the difficulty they had in looking into each other's
eyes at times crystallized into an impossibility;
neither could face the yawning chasm of emptiness
they too often saw there.

***

Zechariah was also resting. He had made good
progress that morning and the three of them were
napping under a leafy tree by the way. He awoke
first and looked about him. He knew these hills and
the path to Jerusalem; he had travelled it many
times before in performance of his priestly duties in
the city. Jerusalem! His heart suddenly moved with
delight. The city never failed to thrill him. Always,
always going up to her awakened hope in him.
There she was, the city of the Great King. There she
was, the promise of hope-filled change, the secret of
the world within her walls. And always there was
that sense of disappointment when he left her; that
failure to meet fundamentally with God, to know
foundational change in that great issue of their lives
which he had seen all too clearly again in Elizabeth's
eyes that morning.

Zechariah looked at his companions still sleeping.
His eyes rested on Azariah and he remembered
their conversation several years before. They had

11

been going up to Jerusalem then and Zechariah had
been confiding in his friend the difficulties he and
Elizabeth were sharing.

"There is still hope, still hope," Azariah had said,
'remember Abraham! He and Sarah had a boy when
the man was a hundred years old. You are not yet
seventy-five!"

"I am sorry my friend, I esteem Abraham but find it
so hard to believe that any such thing will happen
for us."

"Why so? Abraham was an ordinary man like you
or I; he even worshipped other gods beyond the
River. You have served the Lord all your life. Are
you not well placed to receive His blessing?"

"Why should God do for me what he has only ever
done once before? Am I to be another Abraham, the
father of a new nation founded on a miracle from
God? Will Elizabeth bear an Isaac to make us laugh?
I think not. I believe the scriptures but I see no
reason why such a miracle should happen for us."

"Perhaps not the father of a new nation. That
indeed can only happen once. But a father, while
you are both alive, now that is possible still."

"Azariah, you know that Elizabeth and I have lived
on the great names of scripture. How I have
thought upon Manoah and his heavenly visitor.
How I have longed for a Samson with the strength
of God to defeat a Roman legion with a donkey's
jawbone. But all such hopes have proved empty.
Why consider the impossible?"

"With God nothing is impossible Zechariah."

"I know that!" He had snapped back. It was alright
for Azariah, he had children and grandchildren. For
Zechariah though, his family line stopped with him;
a bush in a wasteland. "The hand of the Lord has
gone out against me."
"You should not say that Zechariah."
"Why not if it is the truth! For years we have tried
for children, we have believed, we have fed upon
the scriptures. For some reason though...nothing!
The hand of the Lord has been against us."
"Naomi's words Zechariah, Naomi's words. But the
Lord provided Ruth for her and even Naomi had a
son through the Moabitess."

Zechariah felt frustrated again. Nothing he could
say could shake this man off. Inside he wanted to
scream. Instead they walked along in silence for
some time...actually for a long time. The strange
thing was that the longer they walked the more
nervous Zechariah had become. He was waiting.
Obviously his friend was drawing some piece of
wisdom up from the depths and Zechariah almost
became afraid. Job's companions had sat with him
at the rubbish heap for a week without speaking.
When they finally did say something it was to
accuse Job of hidden sin. Zechariah felt
apprehensive and wanted rather that Azariah
should turn aside. Finally he himself broke that
silence. "I do not understand why; I just don't
understand. We had everything; youth, lineage,
hopes, love. But now we have only old age; the

lineage mocks for this priestly family feels far from God and our hopes are dashed." An angry, despairing tear rolled down his cheek. He didn't say that for years now their love had struggled and stumbled over the rocks and stones of harsh words spoken out of frustration in past years.

"But you still pray!"

"Of course I pray! I am a priest." He took hold of himself and quietened his voice. "But we pray now about other things; our friends and relatives, our rulers, the temple, for peace in our time, for the Messiah to come. We live quiet lives and pray for the hopes of others – their joys, their trials. For our great hope though, we prayed our last prayer together years ago."

Zechariah looked at his friend again; Azariah was stirring. They had not mentioned the subject since and Zechariah almost felt sad. His friend had offered faith and hope but he had turned him away – and had felt guilty for it. He roused himself and stood up, Jerusalem beckoned and hope was rising nevertheless. If not hope for a child still there were other hopes. And one of the greatest for him as a priest was that perhaps this time...this time he would be chosen.

***

The weeks had passed. Elizabeth had visited Judith but each evening ate her bread alone. She was glad no one else had been at the well that afternoon. To be reprimanded by one of the village elders was bad enough, without anyone else knowing about it. She was sure he would not disgrace her by reporting the matter to the council. Besides he knew her situation. Up there on the slope, rain water drained quickly away and left the soil dry. Little would grow there without extra watering anyway but with the dry weather they had had for the last few weeks it was essential if any crop was to be had. She could see the level of the well though and had to admit that, as she debated the matter, she had been generous to herself. Well, no more watering now. The thought worried her. Just a few more weeks and most of the crops would be out of danger. She felt responsible for the garden; she had stayed at home to tend it and now much of the harvest was threatened and without it they faced a bleak year ahead. What news for Zechariah to return to.

Elizabeth lit the lamp and tried to comfort herself by reciting a Psalm.

As the deer pants for streams of water,
So my soul pants for you O God.
My soul thirsts for God, for the living God. (Ps. 42. 1f)

She began to form prayer out of the lines. "Living God you know our need of water. The heavens open at your command. Our souls thirst for you; our garden for your rain."

15

When can I go and meet with God
"Be not angry with me Lord for remaining to tend
the crops while my husband has served you in the
temple. Grant our harvest rain and I vow to you
that I will attend the harvest feast this year in
Jerusalem. I will go and meet with you again in the
temple."

My tears have been my food day and night,
While men say to me all day long,
"Where is your God?"

She did not know what to do with these lines at
first. She struggled; then the waves began to
emerge and crash over her soul once more.

"O living God, why have you forgotten me? You are
compassionate and gracious O God abounding in
and love and mercy."
Tears began to pour down her face.
"I dread the village company O Lord. I cannot walk
at ease among my own people. I hear the voice that
accuses and taunts our faith. 'Where is your God?'
Where are you Lord? How long must I cry? How
long must I feed off tears? How long must I bear
disgrace among men and look down in the presence
of women who could be my daughters? Where is
your love and compassion for me O Lord? The
years of emptiness, O my God, the years of
emptiness!"

She struggled on through the Psalm.

Deep calls to deep in the roar of your waterfalls;
All your waves and breakers have swept over me.

She was crying aloud now; her hands holding her
empty womb. She could hardly speak the words.
She could only think of herself before God.

...a prayer to the God of my life.
I say to God my rock "Why have you forgotten me?
Why must I go about mourning, oppressed by the
enemy?"
My bones suffer mortal agony as my foes taunt me
saying to me all day long,
"Where is your God?"

Elizabeth could not finish the Psalm but sobbed and
sobbed again. Shaken to her core by the tidal wave
that had swept over her, she crawled to her bed
exhausted and surrendered to sleep.

Hannah's prayer of anguish had not even entered
her mind.

***

The messengers stood before the king.
The court was alive with anticipation there was a
distinct buzz in the air.

Magnificent creatures perched and flew about the throne – exotic beasts almost defying description called out to one another.

Before the throne, elders gathered took their seats of honour and did obeisance to the king.

Seers and prophets were there; loyal servants had their own place of honour, some very close to the throne of majesty.

Singers sang and musicians played. The fanfare which accompanied the entry of each dignitary now reached a crescendo as no less a person than the king's son entered the great hall and took his seat. The debate began; a councillor for the prosecution spoke first.

"The man does not deserve the honour" he said, "His heart has often entertained wickedness; he has spoken against your word O king and has doubted your power and kindness. Is this not treason?"

A defendant spoke up; "His is a loyal servant my Lord; one who has served you faithfully for many years. His failings are but those common to men."

"He is not sufficiently interested in the king's honour. He thinks too much of himself and his own glory. Such honour will only puff him up with overweening pride. Not only will it ruin him but it will damage the king's interests."

"He has friends who have petitioned your majesty; they not only vouch for his ability but are there to support him in the execution of the task."

"Your majesty I object. They are but scoundrels who have dishonoured your name. None are to be trusted, none are sufficiently honest, true and good. They will band together against you and bring your name into disrepute once more."

The debate ranged to and fro.

Finally the king's son rose, approached his father and spoke.

"Father, may I be permitted to speak?"

The king looked at him with immense love, "Speak my son." He answered.

"It is true the man has failed us in the past and will almost certainly do so again in the future. We may even now doubt whether he is able to receive this commission or have the necessary good faith to execute it without some element of failure. But, father, the time for your purpose approaches and one must be found who, if not perfectly, will at least adequately serve you in this matter of the herald. I believe we must at least approach him with the task and leave all to his character and to our emissary."

The final word had been spoken. The council for the prosecution shot a glance of pure detestation at the son. There would come a day when he would break this infernal bond and then perhaps his own plans would have their moment of opportunity.

The king, speaking to his son, spoke also to the whole court, "The man has been long tested and tried. He has proved himself, if not entirely dependable, at least partially so. The emissary has observed him and brings a positive report. We shall take the risk!"

The whole court erupted in murmurs of approval which the singers and musicians began to direct in praise of the king, his wisdom and mercy. The prosecution bowed stiffly and moved away his head looking at the floor eyes flashing in anger. The king observed him as he went.
The decision taken, there needed yet one who would take the message.
To whom would the honour fall?
The king called,
"Gabriel!"

***

Zechariah looked at the door and a sigh broke from him.

He had seen that door many times before. He had seen the old door in the old temple. He had seen the elaborate preparations for the re-building of the temple under Herod. He was almost himself re-trained to lay the stones – but even then, was thought to be too old. For decades he had seen that door – but he had never passed through it. He had never entered that room; had never come out to give the blessing to the worshippers outside. Always the lot had gone against him. Elizabeth's womb had been shut; this door of the temple had been shut too. On this tour of duty he had watched again as that door was opened to others; nearly always they were much younger than himself. And each day, however hard he tried to steel himself for the disappointment, it still came as another was chosen. He looked, not without a little envy, as the one chosen took the censor and entered the sacred room - and as the door was closed behind them. But hope had not yet died. The very presence of disappointment showed that. The flame still flickered faintly despite the gusts.

It was nearly the end of their tour of duty. Zechariah had become used again to the bustle of both city and temple. He had worked hard and he longed for his country plot, the shade of his grapevine and the company of Elizabeth again. He was actually presiding at a sacrifice when the lot chose his name to burn the incense. Azariah came over to him and, after he had said the final prayer, informed him of his blessing. Zechariah stumbled at the news, looked at the closed door and shook his head. After so long! Elizabeth will be pleased when he told her; she knew how much it meant to him. He would enjoy telling the rabbi in the village synagogue; an old friend who also knew of his secret desire. It was all so strange, when the censer was put into one hand and the incense in the other he suddenly became nervous, like a little boy. He trembled as the officiating priest, a man far younger than himself, formally instructed him in the correct procedure; something he mused, he knew before this lad was born. The clean robe was adjusted, it was a little too long and he had to walk carefully up the steps towards the door. The doorman opened it before him and closed it behind.

Zechariah stood for a moment in the dim light. Gone was the glare of white stone and gold plate. His eyes adjusted to the softer light of the menorahs as their lamps cast shadows on floor and walls. It was so quiet in here. The noise of animals, of praying of bartering, bleating and lowing were drowned in silence after the great door had been closed. The silence inspired awe; it almost examined the small bustlings of his life. The lamps seemed to scrutinize him, like so many eyes. He moved softly towards the small altar that stood at the far end before the great embroidered curtain. He gazed up at it; its blues, reds and golds almost vanishing into the upper darkness of the ceiling. The final barrier between God and His people. A barrier he could never hope to cross, a door that never would be opened to him in this life. The High Priest alone could make that journey and then only once in each year on that awesome Day of Atonement.

Zechariah gazed upon the curtain for some while and, as he did so, a certain peace and sense of fulfilment filled his own soul for thanks were to be given to God for permitting him entry this far. The supreme moment of his earthly life had come and he uttered a short prayer of personal thanks for this privilege. He then busied himself at the altar laying out the glowing coals and using the golden tongs to gently place the incense upon them. As he did so there was a low hissing sound as the substances were ignited and then clouds of fragrance rose from the altar and were wafted up into the dimness by the heat from coals and nearby menorah lamps.

By now, he knew, a 'direction' would have fallen over the temple courts outside as people in all places would be looking to the central building and a murmur of prayer would have arisen; prayer ascending to God along with the incense. Then he was bathed in the fragrance. Before he had only smelled the scent clinging to the garments of others as they emerged from the temple. Now the clouds seemed to swirl around him and embrace him in tender touch. He drew in a deep breath to savour it all more closely…and coughed. One more piece to go. He lifted it from its golden plate, placed it gently upon the coals and watched as the fragrant cloud emerged from the altar.

A second later all was light before him. His first thought was that he had been too long here and that the great door had been opened to call him out. But the light was before him, emanating from the right and brighter even than the sun outside, yet without pain. He was shocked then astounded as he perceived shape in the light, a human form; a man stood before him, a resplendent man was looking at him from within the light. Nigh on terror gripped

him as the enormity of the event possessed him.
Was he to die at this moment? Had he been too
profane with the holy things? Had this angel been
sent to draw his soul from his body to a judgment
that would condemn him?

In response to his terror he heard words from the
light; "Do not be afraid Zechariah for your prayer is
heard". That he knew his name did not seem
strange; that he was told not to fear was immensely
comforting; that he spoke of prayer was entirely
appropriate for the moment...but that his own
prayer should be heard was unsettling; which
prayer?
"Your wife Elizabeth will bear you a son and you are
to call him John."
The prayer had been heard, THE prayer of his life?
The angel knew of Elizabeth also. A son! But why
the unusual name, John? None of his family went by
that name. Already Zechariah's mind was reeling,
yet further words came to him clear and imprinted
themselves upon his heart,
"You will be joyful and glad." How like Abraham
and Sarah he thought; their joy had erupted in
laughter and so had their son been named.
"Many will rejoice at his birth." Of course, news
would soon spread through the village and family.
"For he will be great in the eyes of the Lord."
"Why?" Thought the priest.
"And he must not drink wine or strong drink."
Samson's parents had been told the same thing.

"And he will be filled with the Holy Spirit even from his mother's womb." This, however, was different from Samson; the Spirit came upon him suddenly...and had left him.

By this time Zechariah's mind was a whirl of thoughts and responses but still the angel spoke. It seemed the Spirit upon the boy was to be like that of Elijah and there was something about turning people's hearts to one another and to God. He could not take everything in and was still wrestling with the first words; Elizabeth will bear a son. This was incomprehensible! For years they had loved and prayed and read and believed but nothing...nothing had ever happened. He wanted, demanded, some assurance;
"By what shall I know this? His words betrayed his tired, empty faith. "I am an old man and my wife is well advanced in years." That was put politely; he suddenly had a picture of them sitting at home in their empty house uttering empty words from hearts drained of hope; they were not just 'old', their ability to bear children was dead.
The angel's next words stunned him.
"I am Gabriel...' Now Zechariah was able to put down a piece of his own. He knew of this angel; it was the same one who had spoken to Daniel the prophet and who had given him such revelations. Zechariah had always admired Daniel and had often pondered the visions he had received. What 'sign'

would this angel give him to confirm that these things will happen?

"I stand in the presence of God." There was a distinct note of frustration in his voice.

"I was sent to speak to you and to announce these good things to you." Zechariah began to feel uneasy and ashamed of himself. This was building up to something and apprehension flashed into his chest. "Look, you will be silent, unable to speak until these things happen because you did not believe my words which will be fulfilled in their time."

Zechariah had his 'sign'! He had spoken rashly and without faith to the very angel who stood before God; but he was not to speak again. He tried to utter some defence, to make some appeal but his voice was closed and no words came forth. Even as he writhed in the frustration of attempting to speak, the angel disappeared, the light vanished and he looked at the coals still glowing on the altar. Lost in thought he took up the censor and made his way between the lines of menorahs to the great door through which he had entered. He lifted the latch and pushed only to be blinded by the light of day that greeted him.

In this light he saw not one but many faces all looking at him and immediately sensed perplexity and frustration. He noticed a chief priest approaching him, a look of irritation in his face. He turned to the people and raised his hand. On the human level this was the supreme moment of his priestly career, to bring the blessing of the intimacy with God he had just been privileged to know, to the crowd of worshippers in the temple courts. All eyes were upon him as his palm faced the people.

But, of course, nothing came out; there was no fruit from his lips, not a sound. He immediately began to struggle, embarrassed; the dreadful silence was confirmed. God would not even permit him to utter the blessing. He looked at the chief priest, pleading for help, but saw extreme anger rising in the face of the other. Priests standing at the top of the steps looked questioningly at him. He felt totally incapacitated and began trying to speak with his hands but sensed he wasn't 'getting though'. Amid tears of frustration and embarrassment he was also unable to hear a voice from the crowd saying "The priest has seen a vision." He tried to gesticulate a message but was encased in a cloud that obscured all audible communication. A hand took him firmly by the arm and led him to the side as another priest performed the blessing. At the bottom of the steps he was led across the court amid a group of priests to a room in one of the gateways where, despite all the consternation and questions, he remained dumb. Released early from his divisional duties he returned home where, in confusion, shame and embarrassment, he remained indoors for days.

Zechariah's life was cut off. He could neither teach
nor pray in public; his duties were at an end. He
was in panic. If he had not believed the angel when
face to face with him, he now had to believe him,
though he saw him no more. If he had misheard or
misunderstood and the boy was not born, then he,
Zechariah, would end his days in utter humiliation;
struck dumb by the God he would soon stand before
in judgment.

Elizabeth was full of concern and questions of
course. Unable to make him hear, she soon learned
to use a rough sign language and, Oh the blessing,
he could still read. They began to keep a writing
tablet and slowly inscribed the more abstract
communications. He set out the vision of Gabriel;
his looks pleading for belief. He wrote down the
angel's words, the second part coming back to him
as clearly as the man of light who spoke them;
"He will turn many of Israel's sons to the Lord their
God; and he will go before him in the spirit and
power of Elijah to turn the hearts of fathers to their
children and the wayward to understanding
righteousness in order to prepare a people for the
Lord."

Zechariah could see that Elizabeth was amazed,
perplexed and not a little frightened over it all. At
first she had been very concerned at the news of his
speech but, apart from this, he seemed well and her
concern had given way to frustration and irritation.

The angel's message was received with joy, tears and unease. Strangely, the miracle of his silence cut through their doubts, and perplexity in turn gave way to resolve.

The renewal of their physical union brought immediate results and Elizabeth was faced with her own miracle. Now she secluded herself and poured over the growing baby in prayer even as Zechariah was sent out to tend the vegetables and fruits. Visitors soon gave up coming to the strange couple's house; Elizabeth would not be seen and Zechariah could not be heard. All sorts of rumours drifted round the village but chiefly, it seemed, Zechariah had had a vision whilst on duty in the temple.

Coming in from the garden Zechariah became used to Elizabeth's praying and re-reading of the tablets on which he had inscribed Gabriel's message. She at least could pray with her tongue; he could only pray without words. Evening after evening he sat in the room, Elizabeth blossoming, praying, giving thanks, praising God; himself wrapped in a cloak of silence.

Occasionally he brooded. He would have liked to share with his wife in praise as he saw her figure round and swell. All their married lives they had waited for this and now he felt as though he could only half enjoy their happiness. There were times when fear sent cold fingers through his soul; had he really heard that penultimate sentence: 'You will be unable to speak until the day that these things come to pass.' He was afraid that he had contrived those words himself; that he would never speak again.

This, however, was not the case.

The whole village seemed to be involved in the birth. The midwives, who needed no help, were deluged with offers of assistance. The village elders sat with their priest as Elizabeth endured the birth. The women gathered at her door. All was relief when the baby's cry came loud and clear and the assessment was proclaimed, 'Mother and son are doing well.' The village children clapped and danced in the street. The old couple's private miracle became a cause for public joy.

Eight days later, at the circumcision, since there had been no communication from the priest, the elders announced that the boy was to be called Zechariah after his father.
"Not so!" Elizabeth's very female voice echoed through the very male group around the baby. All eyes turned in surprise.
"He is to be called John!" Her voice was clear, if shaking slightly with age and emotion.
"This is most unusual." the chief elder examined her, "You have no relatives with that name."

Deaf and dumb, Zechariah himself was oblivious to the consternation. They signalled to him to enquire what the baby's name should be. He signalled back to them asking for a writing tablet and to everyone's amazement wrote, 'His name is...John.' Initial surprise, though, was eclipsed by what then happened, for the next moment Zechariah's voice returned, his tongue was loosed and he, filled with the Holy Spirit, began haltingly at first, but then with greater confidence, to praise God for visiting and redeeming his people and to prophesy over his son.

Later that day, when the festivities were over and the crowd had returned home, Zechariah took a fragment of papyrus and worked on the prophecy that had come to him earlier. He recalled the exact wording and then wrote it down carefully with his pen.

Elizabeth, meanwhile, nursed their son and looked out of the open door at the early melons swelling in their patch as rain fell softly from the sky. The harvest would be good again this year.

2. The Carpenter: Joseph (Part 1)

The carpenter stood back a little from his bench and gazed at his creation. It was indeed the best he had yet made. The wood was now smooth and glowed warmly in the light of the two evening lamps. The carving on the end panel had taken him the afternoon, but had come out well; with that in place the crib was complete. He pushed it with a finger; it rocked gently sending shadows swaying across the walls of the small workshop. He smiled; it was his special contribution.

***

The crowd was seething. Uncertainty, fear and indignation eddied through those who had gathered to hear this latest proclamation from the empire. The official, with two red-crested guards standing beside him, cleared his dusty throat and lifted his voice:

"A decree of your illustrious emperor, Caesar Augustus. That his Excellency may know his subjects better and provide more carefully for their needs; (mutters echoed around the crowd) he has chosen to conduct a census of his entire empire. Each man therefore is to report to his ancestral town with his family, there to be registered. He will need to give details of employment and property owned that his level of tax may be fairly set."

Angry voices were voiced from several quarters, but the raising of just one of the two lances stifled protests to murmurs. Within moments the official was riding out of this town to deliver his proclamation at the next and the crowd broke up into two's and threes For most there would be no physical hardship; they would register right there in Nazareth. For the carpenter though it was a different story; his family had only lived there for the last two generations.

***

Bethlehem was seething, swollen out of all proportions by long gone families returning for the census date. A handful of cottages were tightly shut as newcomers had travelled elsewhere. Both inns were heaving. It was dusk and the first evening stars were twinkling in the gathering darkness as one more donkey padded up the earthen track and into the town. It was led by the carpenter and a girl, of no more than sixteen years, sat uneasily upon its back. They had stopped just below the town to deal with yet another fierce spasm of pain. A bead of sweat from the recent exertion drew a line in the dust that clung to her face. She picked aside a tangle of matted hair. The carpenter, her husband of only three weeks, weary from sleepless nights, blistered from five days walking and still bleeding from another cut, cajoled the reluctant donkey towards the first inn.

"A room? No way mate! We're doubled-up as it is. Try up the street."

The innkeeper pushed shut the door knowing full well that 'up the street' had sent him several families already that evening.

The reply at the remaining inn was the same.

"But they sent us here!"

"How much can you pay?"

"Will a denarius do? It's all we can spare."

"I'm sorry mate I can't help you; not a room available. It's not too cold tonight, you'll have to sleep out in the street – others are, you'll find a corner."

"Friend, help us!" Pleaded the man, "My wife is heavy with child; already she has the pains. Will you let her give birth in the street?"

"What is it Jacob?" A woman's voice sounded from behind the door.

"Two more! He says she's about to bear."

"About to bear! We can't leave them in the street!"

"We're overflowing, you know that. What can we do?"

"What about the outhouse. They could go in there!"

"What are you talking about woman, that's worse than the street."

"It'll give them some privacy, that's what it'll do. Listen to me. You go back inside, I'll deal with this."

The matronly woman brought a lamp and guided them down a narrow alley beside the inn to an outhouse where an old ox was stabled. Several chickens were roosting on the side of its stall. "You'll find straw in that corner, I'll boil some water." she said, then the matron was gone.

The carpenter pitch-forked dung to one side and wearily laboured at preparing a bed. Hardly had he taken his young wife from the donkey and placed her down than her face twisted in agony again in the dim light of the flickering lamp. He rubbed her back to ease the pain out knew it wasn't to be long. Not a moment too soon, the matron returned with a pail of hot water and the inn-keeper's wife become impromptu mid-wife. The baby was delivered and washed. The mother washed and settled. The man watched, with grateful admiration, the efficiency of the matron, and helped when instructed.
"They're not ideal!" She muttered as she swaddled the baby. "I'd have preferred something softer, but I wasn't expecting this." she laughed and caught an enquiring look in the man's face. "My father died a few weeks back. That was the last time I wrapped a body. This was left over from the roll. Not as soft, but they'll do for now. You can buy something better at the market tomorrow. Now...where to put him."
She took the lamp into the one empty stall and busied herself at the trough, pulling fresh hay from a bundle hanging over the side.

"At least he'll be off the ground." She said firmly as she put the newborn into the manger. "Now I must get back." Once again the carpenter thanked her profusely. How grateful he was that he had not had to deliver the child himself on the road. Finally, he himself lay down beside his exhausted wife.

***

But sleep eluded him.

Before long he was sitting with his back to the upright looking around at their lodging lit by the small, sputtering flame of the lamp. A breeze sent the flame flickering once more and the stench of fresh manure stung his nostrils.

Joseph got up and moved cautiously over to the trough where the baby was sleeping. A trough! How he had laboured at the crib. So much had been done in the fading light after the orders of the day had been fulfilled. But it had been done, carved and planed, with care – his supreme love gift to his young wife. For there the baby would be laid; in that crib of love their child of faith would be placed. That was the dream so rudely shattered by the Roman official days after the crib had rocked in its completion on his workbench. For that is where the crib still lay, waiting in desperate hope that they would be back before the baby came.

Now that hope was shattered. The miles of walking
had seen to that. Every jolt, every jar, every foreign
face and stranger's eye; the hope receded as shock
combined with fatigue to drain Mary. Then the
birth pangs had begun and Joseph, exhausted
himself, was whipped into a frenzy of worry and
apprehension that drew from him a desperation to
reach Bethlehem before the baby came. What relief
to see the matron's efficiency. But now, fully awake,
Joseph began to wrestle with his thoughts as he
picked up pieces of shattered hopes.

He had always been an orderly man; his workshop
was a picture of thought and organisation. He
worked with care keeping a tidy bench and floor
even amid the most demanding of tasks. At this
moment, he thought, the crib lay cushioned upon
two layers of neatly spread sacking. But now, as he
ran his hand over the bars of the stable trough
caked with saliva and incidental manure, a splinter
pierced his finger. As he removed it and a small
bead of dark fluid revealed the place, his heart
turned to home. He had prepared it so lovingly for
crib and child, all was in place, all was in order – the
best he could provide. Midwives had been engaged,
soft wrappings procured and loving family and
neighbours were waiting, albeit hesitantly, for the
day. Now that day was here but everything had
been torn away by the icy tentacles of efficient
Roman greed All that could be taken to Bethlehem
was a blanket to cover them at night, some food,

water bottles and their few spare coins for the journey. Joseph gazed in misery at the draughty, stinking, flea-ridden cowshed that was the best he could do for his wife and child now. Dreams of comfort and celebration had evaporated in the heat of the long journey.

What a place for Mary to have her baby!

***

He sat back down and brooded. Well it was her baby wasn't it...her's...and God's...but not his. A flicker of resentment passed over his soul.
"No!" He fought back, "No! I'll not think this!"
But a smooth voice oiled familiar words into his mind.
"God's baby? Oh Joseph!"
"It is. It is God's baby. She saw the Angel Gabriel."
"Oh Joseph. Wasn't Daniel being read in the synagogue at that time? Daniel may have seen Gabriel, but...Mary...is she as great as Daniel? Is a poor peasant girl as notable as the wise adviser to kings?"
"She did see Gabriel. He said the Holy Spirit..."
"The Holy Spirit? The Holy Spirit! Oh Joseph you know that the Holy Spirit left Israel four and half centuries ago. He has never been heard of since. What did this Gabriel have to say? That the baby would be conceived by the Holy Spirit? Joseph, don't you know that that is impossible, unthinkable,

unholy, base...blasphemous? Joseph...babies aren't conceived that way."

Outside the shed, the half-moon was obscured by dark clouds slowly drifting in with the night breeze.

"Joseph, you know how babies are conceived, and, if it wasn't you..."

The carpenter tried to fight back a darkness that encroached upon his soul, coiling about his mind, pressing, constricting.

Whilst the baby was unseen, merely a swelling in Mary, it had been easier to deal with these thoughts. But now, it was flesh and blood, alive, real.

"I saw an angel too!"

"You didn't actually see an angel. You only had a dream about one."

"I...I...had a vision...it was in the night. An angel appeared to me."

"Was that Gabriel too?"

"No...I... I heard no name."

"No name because, Joseph, no real angel."

"No. It was real. I heard a message, 'She will bear a son'. There he is... I even know what name to give him."

"Joseph, you have a real baby to look after now. Now is the time to be real with yourself. You wanted that 'dream' so much. You loved Mary, even after she betrayed you. You hadn't the nerve to divorce her. You saw what you wanted to see and heard what you wanted to hear. Let's not bring God into this."

"It was an angel!"

"Your own pathetic trick Joseph. And now you've married her. For the rest of your life you will bear this shame. A poor, weak man, captured by his own delusions."

"An angel!"

"Oh Joseph, you poor little man!"

Joseph turned away from the lamp and stared into the darkness of a grimy corner, his mind whirling from the assault, his head hung low...hardly a picture of adoration. Everything was so real now. Dreams, visions had had their day...there indeed was the baby...and darkness was staring him in the face.

It was her baby! Her's and...and... . before he knew it a tear had slithered into his beard. Once more he jolted to attention, ready to battle the onslaught...but he was exhausted and within moments other tears had joined the first as his shoulders heaved with the agony of utter failure.

Somewhere, on the other side of town, a dog barked. The carpenter hardly noticed.

He stared into the corner fighting the grief that was rolling in.

"Mary must be protected." he argued.

But Mary already knew.

Despite her own exhaustion and the matted hair sticking to her brow, Mary had awoken and had been watching her husband for the last fifteen minutes. She knew he was wrestling with the doubts again. But now she herself was too drained to whisper more than the simplest of prayers. "God help him!" They had both believed. They had walked together in faith, why again this creeping sense of separation? A tear slid from her eye and dropped onto the blanket spread over the urine-soaked straw.

Another dog barked out of the darkness, this time an angry shout from the town – it worried her. 'Drunks brawling in the midnight streets?' They were all so tired, and with the baby...so vulnerable...no protection of a locked door.

The voices were nearer now. There were men in the street nearby...urgent cries echoed down the narrow alley towards them. Joseph had heard them too. He felt for his stick and moved towards the stable door.

The voices were in the alley itself, coming closer. The carpenter's hand tightened around his wooden staff. Shadows tumbled into the half lit courtyard behind the inn and made for their door. Joseph stepped forward, both hands ready to swing his staff.

"Who's there? What do you want here?" Joseph's voice cut into the night air. He sensed their shock and surprise. He had them on the back foot and advanced towards them.

"A baby." Came a voice out of the darkness...not an angry voice...a trembling voice of an older man. Joseph was about to say, 'There's no baby here'...but that was not true....there was a baby there...and this time it was his turn to be shocked. "What do you mean, a baby?" Was all he could stutter. Joseph's mind reeled again. "Who on earth are you?" He was saying.

But the older, quieter voice spoke up. "Friend, if there is no baby here, just tell us and we'll be on our way!"

"There is a baby here." Joseph's hand motioned but his voice hardly seemed his own. The simple truth was spoken almost as in a dream.

"In a manger?" Came a cry from the simple shadow.

"You can't come in here!" Joseph barked out his defensive screen.

"Joseph, I think it will be alright." That was Mary. She had joined her husband and held the lamp behind him.

Rough hands pushed passed the carpenter. Shadows emerged into the shed and became men. Then a gasp.

"He's here!"

"It's him. Come and take a look at this mates. Sorry Miss! He's over here in the manger."

Suddenly the little shed felt crowded. Another lamp was lit, then another and were held up to get a better view.

"And look...swaddling bands alright. They ain't no cloths you'd wrap a baby in."

"Just like he said, just like he said." Came the simple voice of one of the younger men. "A baby, wrapped in swaddling cloths and lying in a manger."

Joseph's hand tightened around his staff again as he stepped forward to take control and confront these intruders a second time. "What are you talking about? Who said?" He almost shouted at them.

"The man in white." Said the simple voice.

"The angel!" The older man's voice was full of certainty.

"Angel?" Joseph's stick fell to the ground as he searched the old man's eyes in the dim light. "What do you mean...angel?"

"We were with the sheep, guarding them. Then from nowhere he appeared."

"All shining he was, sir! Shining white."

 "There was light all around us..."

"We was scared stiff mate, all of us." The big man hadn't spoken before. "I thought it was the end. We all dropped to the ground waiting for the blow to strike..."

"But no blow came" the old man reminded him.

"I was driven out of me wits." The big man interrupted, "We all were...shaking like leaves, we were."

"But he, that is the angel sir, he told us not to fear..."

"Seth, let me alone to tell the man." The older shepherd quietened him.

"You tell 'im then Matthew."

"The angel told us he came with good news, great joy, a Saviour...born in David's town, Christ the Lord. He gave us a sign... 'You will find the baby wrapped in swaddling clothes and lying in a manger.'"

"We had to come and find him." The big man interrupted, "We had to leave the sheep mister. We had to come and see the king."

Joseph's mind was still reeling; he could not grasp the details. "An angel you said?"

"Yes sir...but then there were lots more." Seth was suddenly in full flow. "On the hills sir, the valley was full of 'em. But it was only our valley you see, the others, that is the other shepherds, didn't see them. But they were there sir, singing they were...they filled the sky...and he, that was the first one sir, he said we'd find the king in a manger an' all, and he'd be wrapped...well...just like he is sir.

"M...More...more angels?"

"Yes." Matthew's voice now shook with emotion. "No sooner had he spoken, than they began to appear. Hundreds upon hundreds...rank upon rank...the sky was full...it was like daylight...they were singing. Oh how they sang. They sang the glory of God. They kept repeating it 'Glory to God...glory to God in the highest'. I found myself mouthing it. Then 'Peace on earth' they sang, 'Peace on earth to men of goodwill.' Rank upon rank there were... the hosts of heaven...all around us."

Joseph just looked at Matthew...speechless, swaying, looking deeply into the old man's watery eyes. Then, in a moment, the carpenter embraced the old shepherd and hugged him like he was his father, fresh tears rolling down his own cheeks. The others gathered around him and comforting hands were laid upon his heaving shoulders. After some time Joseph drew back wiping his cheeks with his hands, still looking at Matthew.
The old man spoke. "This hasn't been easy for you has it my friend."
"No!" Joseph's voice quivered with the admission.
"The baby?" The old man enquired.
"Not mine." Joseph admitted, "Fathered by the Holy Spirit."
Matthew shot a glance at Mary. She nodded but sought the old shepherd's assent.
He turned back to Joseph and looked him straight in the eye, "Let me ask you just one question. Are you a son of King David?"
"A descendant" admitted the carpenter.
"But...of course," after a moment's reflection the old man's verdict came with a note of sheer amazement in his voice, "...of course. 'To you in David's town...'"
He was remembering what the angel had said. "'...is born...Christ...the Lord.' THE Son of David."
He looked deeply into the carpenter's eyes.
"No. No...you'll not be the father.

But I tell you..." he added, "...you be a father to him."

3. The Shepherds

"The evening began like any other; the last watering of the day, then leading up to the folds on the valley side, cursing the stragglers nibbling at the path edges, the odd warning stone flung near their backs to move them on, the counting in and cursory glance to check that each was sound, before gathering wood for the fire. Well worn paths, hearths that seemed eternal, patterns as ancient as Abel. The boiling of the flesh and the grains in the pot. The murmurings from the flock dying down as animal after animal chewed or slept. Tales told over the broth and barley bread, rough humour too as the wine vinegar flowed from the skins. The evening began like any other.

The night too. Sure the town was busy, busier than usual; those Romans and their obsession with numbers and organisation. Military technology riding roughshod over the sensitive souls of men, bearing the thorns of irritation and misery. At least out here in the quiet hills one could feel alone, away from their grasp – even if it were only a mirage of freedom.

Yes it was good to be out under the silent stars, hidden by the folds of the hills from the restless lamps of the bulging town below.

The embers died down amid the flints and then one by one the small group began to break as we dispersed to our folds, to our blankets and to our doorways there to settle as living gates between our flocks and the predators of the night. That night had begun like any other.

But in a moment we were snatched from a dew damp dark reality to the vibrancy of a dream gleaming.

Who saw him first I do not know, but that scream echoed up and down the valley. Animals started, bleating and stamping. Fellows reached instinctively for clubs and slings; in an instant all were alert. But, as soon as sticks were in hands, as soon again they were clattering to the stones, knuckles white as men stared up the valley at the man in light. Mouths agog, speechless, hearts melting with terror as fellows sank to their knees. Wave after wave of fear pulsated through hardened frames; we drew back from him as he advanced down the valley path. Synagogue attendance had told us all too plainly what this meant. The power of the ancient writings broke upon us with the force of contemporary urgency; the angel of the Lord was come to gather us to a judgement for which each man knew in his heart he was ill-prepared. Written on ashen faces was the faithlessness of each one.

Overwhelmed and gripped with the proximity of
eternal judgment our hearts froze as we watched
the approach; until the man spoke. There was no
shout, but the message played upon our ears for
moments retrieved from eternity. His words
entered every soul like warm breath; "Don't be
afraid!" Our hearts clutched at the syllables. We
had, each one of us, every reason to fear, yet from
the vision issued words of succulent peace whose
flavour we savoured again and again with our
minds until our raging hearts were stilled and the
question formed, 'Why ever not?'

He spoke again. Information and invitation mingled
in words measured, rhythmic with the quality of
poetry;
'To you' – that is us.
'In David's town' – that is Bethlehem below.
'Is born today' – right now, tonight.
'A saviour' – our whole need in this moment!
'Who is' – time slowed as ancient names raced
through our minds – Gideon, Jepthah, David, Joshua,
Moses!
'Who is...Christ the Lord.' The last phrase
thundered into our bellies like a ball of fire. Ancient
accounts, age old prophecies, promises worn with
time and covered with the sands of recent
disturbing history. The Messiah – born?

Our crowded minds seemed to have little room for
his next words which spoke of...signs."

***

The carol singers began assembling in the hall. There was a distinct atmosphere of expectation. This was to be a special concert and all were aware of its immense significance. Royalty would be there and not a hair must be out of place. They had often sung before in the presence of the king and though each concert had a life of its own, rendered unique by the vibrant atmosphere of His Majesty, there were also those times when the event itself added its own lustre and made the rendition particularly memorable. Such was now the case. Though the King himself could not be there, all knew that his intense interest would ignite the atmosphere with his presence; his ambience would be tangibly felt and, upon his throne, he would listen carefully to all reports of the concert. For this rendition was to be held in a neighbouring realm and the singers were to be His ambassadors.

The choir leader counted in the members. Robes were checked and adjusted and locks of hair were moved away from faces. A sudden silence indicated preparation and anticipation. All eyes focused upon the Cantor. He swallowed, drew a deep breath and, began to give the opening notes, adjusting each to perfection until it was taken up and echoed back to him first from the sopranos and altos, then from the tenors and bases. The symphonic blend of 'warm-ups' told the leader that all were in fine voice and especially responsive at this time to fellow singers and to the conductor. Several minutes later, with voices warm and vocal chords supple, a second silence descended. Then the leader spoke.

"You are all aware of the importance His Majesty attaches to this concert. Not only will it be a display of His glory power and might, it will also be one given in a hostile realm. As such it will ring out a message to the enemy that his days are numbered. It will also proclaim to those whom he forcefully subjugates, that there is near hope of the end to their oppression. This message His Majesty particularly wishes to be communicated with clarity and authority. Stay, together, physically and vocally knowing that The Emissary is with us at all times. The way has been cleared and the stage prepared. All that remains for us now is to offer ourselves once again for the display of His glory. Cantor, the new song please."

The Cantor again gave the notes and the new anthem was rehearsed a final time. As voices were raised, the hall began to echo until the whole was filled with the sound and began to vibrate at the crescendo. They were ready.

Immaculately attired gate-keepers lifted latches and swung open the huge doors. Line upon line, the choir approached the portal and entered through.

Leaving the shimmering eminences of His Majesty's palace they dropped away from the light and fell with increasing speed towards the darkness below. From the third, down into the second and finally the first. The atmosphere here cloyed with the suffocating presence of the enemy hordes. The choir felt it tangibly as they fell through it, and claws, jaws and swords sought to break in and engage the incoming choir in battle.

But, the vortex that had been created, held and, led by the basses, the whole ensemble, like flames of fire, plummeted towards the prize jewel. As the host approached, the realisation that they were but the anticipation of that far greater multitude gripped them again. They alone would carol the Great Prince's first commission, but for his return and glorious enthronement they would merely vanguard with victory songs the mighty army that would at that time be in attendance.

The jewel became visible now, half lit by its star, and the basses had to restrain themselves from a deep rumble of rejoicing. Circling the orb they passed around to its shaded side and the great landmass known as Asia, thence to its south western point at the hinge of the continents, the centre of the earth. Invisible wings unfurled to the ether and, like swans descending towards a lake, the ranks slowed until they merely hovered, poised. A chieftain had preceded them and was even now addressing the audience – a quartet of Adam's shabby sons, yet also four images of their own Majestic King. At a signal, the curtain went up and voices thundered into the cool midnight air.

***

 "The man in light had hardly spoken when singing filled the valley as from an army eager from victory. Our eyes strained to see the voices as wave upon wave tumbled over tingling ears. Then, I can only say 'as it were', our eyes were opened and we saw. Troops, rank on rank of them from valley side to valley side shimmering in glorious light, their praise pulsating through the silence even as their glory shone through the clear night.

I didn't look at my fellows in that while. I knew they were as amazed as I; transfixed by this compelling sight. Wonder filling our bellies; bodies hardly able to contain the flow of emotion and awe. Tears smudged on dusty cheeks, streaming down into greying beards as all in a man was focussed as never before on the vision before us. Adoration and praise was drawn from our bellies as we began to mumble in concert with them:

Glory to God in the Highest
And peace to His people on earth,
To those who receive His grace.

How long we were there I cannot say; an eternity it seemed, yet, as the vision before us had built up, so gradually it was dismantled. The army rose, ascending amid the praise, the shimmering glory lifted...and receded. Our straining necks arched to hold the last glimpses of sight as the shining ones ascended on invisible wings, the cloud of light dispersing and melting into the heavens. We continued looking but the last was gone; our gaze was reflected by the cold stars twinkling out of the clear sky; the last strains carried away by the night breezes.

Men still sobbed, their faces now in the dust. But even these heavings subsided and, one by one, we pulled ourselves to our feet, strained yet exhilarated. As we stumbled towards each other to grasp an arm or rough collar, our conversation echoed with the urgency of our response. Through grimy tears we pressed the demand on our fellows to leave the flocks and go down into the town to find the new-born. In moments we were in agreement and tumbling together down the valley in the half moonlight. Our conversation was filled with the visitation, the magnificence of the light and the words of the first...angel; yes, angels, that's what they were, we all agreed.

We rounded the spur and looked up the next valley fully expecting to see others rushing towards us carried along by the same sight. But all was quiet.

All was still. Everything looked so…ordinary…so
menacingly normal. Shem picked his way up to the
first fire for news. As the three of us stood there
waiting for his return, excitement receded. Chatter
died as we waited for confirmation of the visit to
further strengthen our resolve. The darkness stole
upon our souls; conversation became inanely
commonplace.

A noise nearby startled us. Shem returned but his
excitement had given way to perplexity. We
demanded news. Had they seen the angels? Are
they coming, or already ahead? He shook his head.
'The watchman cursed me for waking him and told
me I was a drunken fool for my story.' We looked at
each other for a moment in confusion and a feeling
of unease hovered on our dark gazes. But…let them
to it…we had to go on!

As we stumbled ahead we examined the words we
had heard.
'Christ the Lord!'
Even as we spoke the words the darkness seemed
to echo them into our ears as fantasy. What were
we doing? The town was sullen with the
compulsion of registration and restless with the
press of foreigners and here we were tripping
towards it expecting to find the Messiah. The
Messiah promised a thousand years and more and
still awaited with aching burdened hearts. We were
to find the Christ! But why us? Why should the

Almighty tell a bunch of nobodies? And the sign the angel had spoken of? Consider it again. The new-born would be found lying in a trough wrapped in the bandages of a corpse. As we approached the 'city', this double promise that would confirm the truth of our visitation, of our quest and of the child, began to laugh inanely at our reason.

We stopped on the outskirts of town suddenly unsure of what to do next. Coarse laughter, and hollow, drifted across from a house nearby where shadows obscured the slight light of an oil lamp. We knew Bethlehem was angry at many of its intruders and they were angry at Bethlehem's menial hospitality. Some of these would be 'sons of David' returning to the birthplace of their royal ancestor, but, far from enjoying palatial receptions, they were crammed into hastily prepared hovels. How the mighty had fallen! For some, drink and bitter humour was the immediate consolation for gross inconvenience. Bethlehem's seething did not bode well as a reception for our strange quest, but on we must go.

To be in a trough the new born had to be in one of the outhouses...but which one?

Our muttered prayers to the Almighty for guidance and preservation were not immediately answered. Dogs barked, challenges and curses were flung through the night at us as we stumbled around the

sheds our feet rapidly reeking of dung and urine
while in stable after stable the only living things
that greeted us were the nodding heads of oxen or
the squawk of a hen woken by our intrusion and
frightened...of course. Of course...well what did we
expect to find in these manure encrusted lean-to's?
Did we expect to find a glorious king...God's
Messiah...the saviour and crown of Jacob's
descendants? Fool's...deluded fools we felt as into
another dark hut we searched for the king. Only
darkness and the sweaty grunting of an ass greeted
our quest, its silly grin mocking us from the
shadows. Again we moved on consoled by the
knowledge that this challenge must soon end.

Bethlehem could have only so many mangers!

Then, quite suddenly it was, everything changed.
We had passed one of the bulging inns where a
snapping dog strained at us from the end of a taught
rope and another curse was flung at us from a
nearby room. We had turned down an alley and
were approaching the outhouse when, dimly
through the split planks, we saw a lamp was
burning; someone was in there! Slithering through
a patch of slime we entered the courtyard and made
our way towards the opening. A challenge cut
through our hushed but expectant chatter,
'Who's there?' The voice was insistent yet weary,
bold but it betrayed exhaustion and not a little fear.
He spoke again, 'What do you want here?' I saw the

man more clearly now, a staff in his hand ready to swing at my skull.

Our business? The demands of reason. Before I knew it I spoke, 'A baby.' Such 'business' sounded ridiculous at that hour. Other words, but then the latch closed it seemed.

'You can't come in here!'

However, still hope, a woman's soft, tired voice sounded from behind him. 'Joseph, I think it will be alright.'

The man, Joseph, stepped back and aside from the lamp whose small flickering suddenly blinded our eyes accustomed as they were to straining in dark corners. The scene was simple, squalid, yet in measure familiar by now. An ox lolled at its tether, a donkey, its lip curled round the hay net on the wall. But now also a woman, exhausted, hair matted from the sweat of exertion lying beneath a blanket on a heap of assembled straw. The ox belched and ejected. The stench of its urine drifted towards the lamp. The man, Joseph, motioned towards a wall. What?

'There is the baby.' He said simply.

We peered towards the rough timbers. Seth reached for the lamp and drew it in front of us. There, hammered into the planks and uprights was the ox's manger, the gaps in its slats worn and widened by teeth and rasping tongue. Dung caked

the planks below it but it itself was clean, even
washed by the beast's saliva. The animal followed
us with its eyes as we approached its trough.
Tethered in the second stall, it watched us move to
its feeding point. I searched the dim scene and
indeed, there, in the manger, a bundle of white
cloths reflected the soft light of the lamp and a new-
born's lips puckered. Other lamps were lit and
illuminated the scene

In a manger! Well there he was, and wrapped in
cloths – swaddling cloths – they were there too; the
coarse linen of the entombed wound fast around the
delicate skin of the new-born. Suddenly all the
harshness of the sight revealed by the lamp hit me
with force. What an unwelcome entry into the
world of men this child had had. Thrown out of the
town, its bed nailed to cross timbers rising from the
dung and wrapped like a stillborn; dead in birth.
Tears welled up in my eyes. Complex tears of
compassion, of sympathy for this mean small family,
compelled to such lowliness by the organisational
demands of the powerful. Yet they were also tears
of joy for the little corpse was yet alive its lips
seeking its mother's milk. Remembrance of the
glorious visitation in the valley above found
confirmation in the double sign below; the
apparition in the hills found reality in David's town.
The man in light had spoken and the truth of his
words was enfleshed before our eyes. We could
touch the bandages, feel the trough and see with

our own eyes the new-born before us. This baby then was the Messiah, the Christ, the Lord, the Saviour, born in David's ancient city this day.

Seth and the man began talking of the angels. Joseph wanted details of our encounter, and Seth being a bit simple, I joined in and gradually excitement yielded to exactment. Suddenly the man broke and began to weep. For a moment I knew not what to do and searched for a reason for his tears. It was as he held onto me that I felt myself in his place. Here was Messiah's father knee-deep in squalor.

But as I pondered those words 'Messiah's father', they did not sit comfortably with me and I had to question him about this. No. he was not the father. Either the woman bore immense guilt...or...what? Had she born one conceived by the Almighty? The angel left me in no doubt and a simple question confirmed it. Messiah, we all knew, would be the Son of David and here was Joseph a descendant of the great king indeed. My own mind was still racing, surging forward on waves of joy. This meagre sight confirmed the reality of our visitation – no need to doubt, question or fear anymore. Like a warm day in the perfume of meadows I could bask in the light we had been shown, simply enjoy it, receive it, laugh with it and weep with its immensity.

It was time!

This new-born, lying swaddled in a manger, was indeed Christ, our long awaited Messiah. Promises echoing along paths worn through valleys of time, had crescendoed in the unspeakable rejoicing of the angels' song.

'Why ever to shepherds?' ...but then I might as well ask...
'Why ever in this crutty invested lean-too?'
'Why?'

Surely a wisdom beyond my grasp. But...a wisdom substantiated and true. Two incredible sights, one incredible, the other squalid, yet clasped in solid agreement and, arching over the exhausted couple, proclaimed 'He has arrived!' God's glory, when accepted, radiating peace into the troubled, storm-tossed hearts of men.

Through our hearts had stormed the events of this night. We were men shaken, but now, seeing this, a joy-filled peace shone through us. We were recipients of God's unmeritable generosity. In a few short hours we had been moved from the humdrum, to the brink of fearful judgement, to reprieve, to the adventure of an outrageous quest, through the cynicism and abuses of an indifferent untouched world to the place where heaven's word touched earth's squalor and inflamed us with vitality.

Then, suddenly a cold chill swept through us. The flocks, our cares, our living - the fold doors lay open, anything might have happened. We gave our farewells to the couple and left the town for the hills. By the time we reached our valley we were in panic, years of wages, chances of labour clawing at our minds. What on earth had possessed us to leave the flocks unguarded? We rushed to the nearest fold expecting empty walls or worse the remains of a flock ravaged by the night beasts. We peered in but saw only woolly waves...all were within, asleep; Seth counted for they were his. Asa's fold too; all present. I clutched at the hope that mine would also be there. They were, an occasional ewe opening a puzzled eye sensing a strange urgency. All there! We had been hours, half the night or more, yet not one was missing, all were at peace, even resentful at our apprehension. Such a peace too reigned in the valley; we now began to sense it.   All was quiet, unusually silent. Our perceptions searched up and down the valley for danger or threat, but none was present, just the peace...a peace, perceptible almost as a presence, as though some hidden shepherd sat quietly watching over our flocks...over us. Dawn was breaking over tired minds now but...was it too much to fancy that some formless shepherd had both kept watch here and had led us down to Bethlehem, to drink living waters from its ancient well?

It was this latest miracle that enervated us out of exhaustion to one final consideration. Why had the angels come to us and not to those in nearby valleys? Why wasn't the whole town gathered to welcome the Messiah during the hours of daylight? That would have been far more convenient in many ways. The reason, we soon decided, was not so hard to see. God wanted it that way. He had wanted only a small group to know and his revelation had been given to us in the secrecy of night. But why to shepherds? The key to this question was that quiet presence guarding our flocks. We had been invited to celebrate the birth of one of our own. Shopkeepers gather at a birth to a shopkeeper, magistrates at a birth to a magistrate; we shepherds had been gathered to a birth of a shepherd, to the nativity of the Messiah, THE Shepherd of His people Israel. But unlike the fanfares that accompany the birth of other babes we did not noise this abroad; a flash of light spitting the darkness, this was God's secret, and we were bound to Him to keep it.

Between ourselves words were often spoken...

...but not a thing about our night adventure was said to anyone else."

4. The Prophet: Simeon

The old man shuffled down the narrow alleyway. A cold wind lifted the debris of straw and sent icy fingers through the tears in his cloak. He drew the garment around him, stepped carefully around the offal in the street and clutched at the bundle under his arm. It would never do for that to fall here. He turned left down another squalid backstreet then out onto one of the main thoroughfares. Avoiding carts, carriers and donkeys struggling under loads, he made his way up the incline towards the temple and crossed the street. A squad of soldiers marched towards him, the steel of their spears glinting in the cold morning sunlight. He drew back into one of the shop doorways but still felt the push of the captain's rough hand.

'You there, out of the way!'

He stumbled, held fast to the bundle and thought to complain, but already they were past him and moving confidently down the street, traffic moving aside. He stepped gingerly out of the doorway and began up the hill again feet dragging through the rotting vegetables beside a market table. Left again and round under the temple mount, a tree marking the boulevard of the affluent. He crossed the street once more, mounted the steps and knocked.

Moments later a maid opened the door.

"Shalom! The master's coat." He held the bundle up for the girl to see.

"Shalom! Wait here!" She stepped back into the house. The master called over his shoulder and came to the door.

"Your coat sir. The tear, it is mended."

"Ah yes," he inspected the garment, "and a good mend too Simeon. How much do I owe you?"

"One denarius."

"Are you sure? A day's wage for an hour's work?"

"That was our agreement."

"Come now, surely half at the most!"

"Your word sir."

"I do not recall promising such extravagance Simeon. Here, a half, and be content with your good fortune. This should buy you cloth for the tears in your own cloak and bread for the week I should think."

"But the cloth; it took me a morning to find the match, and the stitches, you can hardly tell..."

There was no use in arguing. Caleb was a hard man. He would have that burley servant push him away again if he did not accept and the court would not back the old man. He took the coins and began back up the road. The door shut behind him and a shout came from within the house.

Across the street at the top of the hill and into the market. Three cubits of cloth and a warm loaf and the coins were gone. The thought of freshly baked bread cheered him though. He turned right into the alleyway and the backstreets towards his room. At the end of the passage a commotion filled the air

with vehemence. 'O Jerusalem, what have you for
me now?' He thought.
"No money, no room!" The voice ricocheted
towards him.
"Mercy, is there no mercy?" The frantic female
voice was shrill.
"You are a wicked woman! You entertain men and
hide your takings."
"Liar! You insult me in the hearing of my children."
Simeon could see them now, three of them clutching
at her skirts.
"Enough take your business elsewhere!"
"Business! I have no business, not the sort you say.
I have no money and you have no pity."
"Learn a trade then, sell at the market, but no
money no room!"
"Where am I to stay with my children? Where am I
to sleep?" She was in tears now.
"If it's a bed you want Sarah!" He leered at her.
She lifted her head, eyes flashing and spat at him.
"When the Messiah comes justice will be done!"
He laughed. "One day you may be grateful for the
offer." He turned and slammed the door.
Simeon had been rooted to the spot. But as she sat,
crumpled in the street, shoulders heaving with sobs,
he approached her.
"Did he call you Sarah?"
"My name", she said, her long hair sticking to her
cheeks.
He waited for her sobbing to subside; "What will
you do now?"

"Now? I do not know what I shall do! My husband is gone."

"You husband is no more?"

"He was a good man but hot tempered. He died two days after the Roman patrol beat him senseless. That was three weeks ago." She added.

"You have no money?"

"My brother, he has a little, but he drinks the wine. Yesterday he said he had none for me."

"The man, he said..."

"The man is a liar!" She looked at him eyes ablaze...yet also beseeching belief.

Simeon paused. "What will you do now?"

"I do not know. I can cook and clean; I can wash and mend, but I only have one brother." She wept again this time uncontrollably for several moments.

He waited again, kneeling beside her. One child stroked her head, the other two looked silently at him. He caught their eyes. "Here is warm bread;" he said, "the children are hungry." He paused again, "'A lady by the name of Martha lives up from Siloam. She may be able to help you."

"You...you give us your bread!"

"Tomorrow I'll buy more...perhaps." He added.

"Thank you, yes thank you Sir. A good man. 'Martha' you say, up from Siloam?"

"I don't know if she can help you; it is just a thought."

"You are a kind man. How can I repay you."

"No payment, go to Martha." They stood up and she turned to go, children at her skirts. "Sarah..."

"Yes."
"The Messiah will come!"
She looked at him from the corner of her eye.
"I am an honest woman, I do not lie."
But he was neither judging nor accusing. Now her
eyes bore into his; he turned his head from her
stare. "They say he will come", She sighed and her
lips curled, "why doesn't he come now?"
"He will come...soon."
"Soon! How do you know?"
But he turned away and left her to lead her flock
towards the market.

Simeon sat in his room. There was still a little meal,
water in the pot and a few sticks beside the hearth.
He would light a fire and cook. Half an hour later
and the thin porridge was slipping down,
supplemented by several scraps of dried bread. Not
exactly a feast, but his soul fed on the thought of
Sarah's children devouring the warm bread while
she and Martha sat and planned a way of hope for
the destitute family. Martha was a good woman,
she would know what to do.

Simeon sat in his room. He could still see Sarah's
penetrating eyes and hear her incredulous voice
"How do you know?"

**

About sixty years before

**

68

"Simeon! Simeon! Where are the goats?"
Simeon started at his father's words.
The goats. The goats! They've strayed again! Where
were those creatures?
"They were here a minute ago!" He fumbled for
words, his father bearing down upon him.
"Have you been sleeping again?" His father's voice
was furious and accusing.
"N...No! I...I..."
"Well, where are they?"
Just then a bleating from behind told him they were
in the ravine further up the mountain.
"They're here father! They're all alright!" He didn't
know this of course but it deflected his father's
wrath for the moment. He leapt up and ran behind
the bluff eager to get away from his father,
desperate for the flock's safety. What had he been
doing? Had he been asleep? There they were! He
began counting; two missing! Another bleat beyond
the next bluff; Simeon ran towards the sound and
the cliff he knew lay beyond it. One creature was at
the edge bleating in alarm; Simeon stopped then
walked slowly towards it. The goat backed away
still bleating. He stopped again; if it were to slip!
He called gently, the small animal settled and
allowed him to slip his crook round its leg and pull
it away from the drop. He caught it up in his arms
as another bleat came from below; immediately the
kid began its bleating again. The mother was down
there! He peered over the edge and saw her on a

ledge a few cubits below struggling in a bush. He
felt his father's hand on his shoulder.
"Not too near the edge my son." The voice was calm
and gentle, the hand guided him to safety.
"The mother's down there; she's caught."
"Take the kid back to the flock; let us see what can
be done."

Simeon tied the kid to a sapling, returned and
watched as his father summed up the situation then
slinging the coil from his shoulders tied one end
around the base of a tree the other loosely around
his waist and over one shoulder. Playing out the
rope he descended to the ledge and gently
disentangled the frightened creature from the bush.
Taking off his headpiece he wrapped it under the
goat's belly, knotted it above, passed the rope under
the knot and tossed the end to Simeon.
"Pull gently, ease her over the stones and
brushwood." He said and took up the sling. Talking
to her all the while he lifted the animal above his
head and let his son take the strain. A few struggles
but she was soon back over the edge out of the sling
and bounding towards her kid. Simeon lowered the
rope back down to his father and watched him tie
up and climb back up the crag. Now surely, with the
danger over, his father's anger would find
expression.
"She seems not to have suffered." He eased grit out
of one eye and brushed blood, his own, away from a
cut in his arm. As he walked passed the boy the

hand was on his shoulder again but again his voice came gently.

"Look after the goats son. They are our living."

Moments later, with his father beyond the bluff, the strain began to fade and Simeon took several deep breaths.

"Oh Lord! I didn't even pray."

From where he could not tell, but a voice answered and words came to his mind, a whisper yet reverberating around his chest and head;

"You will not die before you have seen the Saviour."

Simeon stood there panting; looking at the edge of the cliff.

***

"Rabbi. Who is 'the Saviour'?"

Nathan squinted at the young man. His eyesight was not as good as it used to be. Was that Simeon asking the question? So it appeared.

"Well now, the Saviour," he began, "well, the Saviour is the king, he is...he is the Messiah, the one, who when...when he comes, will save his people Israel. When he comes he will deliver his people from their enemies and he will sit upon the throne of his father David. He will bring justice and peace to Israel and so Israel will be comforted. Also he will be mighty and wonderful and...and I ask myself, I ask myself, 'Why should Simeon ben Jemuel be wanting to know this?'"

The other boys and young men, sitting at the feet of the village Rabbi, looked at Simeon. Simeon did not know what to say. The words had tumbled from his mouth and now seemed to scatter like a flock of goats driven to pasture. He did not know which way to turn.

"I...I...heard of the Saviour the other day and..."

"And who spoke to you of the Saviour? Was it your father?"

"Well...no, it was not my father."

"Was it your uncle?"

"No it was not my uncle."

"Your mother?"

"No it was not my mother."

"Was it one of your goats Simeon?" His rival Shaul put in. The other boys laughed, Simeon's face flushed and the Rabbi was distracted in dealing with Shaul. School could not end soon enough for Simeon that day, but as the group dispersed Nathan drew him aside.

"And so, your answer to my question."

"Your question sir?"

"The one who spoke to you of the Saviour."

Simeon still had no plan of retreat. The words tumbled again.

"I was in the hills the other day, my father rescued a mother goat. I heard a voice saying that...that..."

"That...what?"" The old man coaxed, neither mocking nor angry.

"That I should not die before I had seen the Saviour."

The old man peered into his eyes, searching for truth.

"Many of us have desired to see the Messiah young man. These are hard times for Israel. The Roman general Pompey...and the temple...hard times...and many long for the Saviour to come...but a voice you say?"

"Yes, like a voice...words came to me."

"Many people hear voices my son."

"Rabbi."

"Yes my son."

"You have told us that the Lord spoke by His Spirit to the prophets."

"This is true, in former times the Lord spoke by His Spirit to the prophets."

"Does He still speak to people by His Spirit today Rabbi?"

"Maybe. But His Spirit has not inspired a prophet for four hundred years now. The Lord may still speak to the High Priest. Is it that you think He has spoken to the son of a goatherd in the Arabah?"

"I...I...I do not know what to say. Was not David a shepherd?"

"David was a shepherd and also David was a great king. Are you another David, Simeon?"

"No...No...I am not a David Rabbi."

Nathan's eyes followed him as he left the school. The old Rabbi was deep in thought.

***

"I do not understand you Simeon!"
His father's look was one of anger, grief and
perplexity.
"You leave your father and mother, your brothers
and sister. You leave your village, the young men
you have grown up with. You leave your land and
flocks, your very livelihood and all for a dream fired
by the heat of the Arabah."
Lemuel was not desperate. His eldest and youngest
sons had no such ideas. They would stay and the
flocks would prosper under their care. They would
support him in his old age. But he was grieved that
his middle son was determined to go.
"I must leave father. When the Messiah comes it
will surely be to Jerusalem and I must be there to
see him."
"There you go again; 'When the Messiah comes!' We
have waited hundreds of years for the Messiah to
come...Ah...but we have been through all this
before. Your voices on the desert wind."
"I may be wrong father, but it is the desire of my
heart. It has become my worship of the Lord."
"Do you worship God my son by breaking your
mother's heart?"
"I will see you every year at Passover father. When
you come to Jerusalem for the feast you must stay at
my house. I will be a merchant and become very
rich. You will stay in luxury. You and mother will
be very proud of me."

"Ha! What does a goat boy know of buying and selling, of cloth, or spices or jewels?"
"I will learn father." But in his heart Simeon knew that he would have much to learn.
"Where will you stay?"
"Rabbi Nathan has a cousin who lives there. I am to stay with him until the Feast."

***

Simeon was to stay with the Rabbi's cousin for two years. During that time the Roman general Crassus plundered the Temple's wealth before proceeding east to his death at the hands of the Parthians.

Simeon found work at the market, at first cleaning up around the stalls, then running a stall of his own. Earthenware vessels gave way to cloths but he was never a very successful stallholder. He built up a knowledge of fabrics though and developed skill as a tailor that, for a while, brought a modest living. He was able to marry and provide dowries for both their daughters.

Jerusalem went through further trouble. Antipator, whom Julius Caesar had made procurator, rebuilt the city's walls. When Caesar's assassin, Cassius, came east to collect money, Antipator wisely provided for him but shortly after was himself murdered. Three years later Simeon witnessed the Parthian invasion of Judea and takeover of

Jerusalem. Hyrcanus the high priest was mutilated and Antipator's eldest son committed suicide. Antipator's younger son Herod escaped to Rome where he was made King of Judea. He had to fight for his throne though and this ended three years later with his re- taking of Jerusalem.

Simeon's family only narrowly escaped the Roman butchery. His elder daughter survived then and was married two years later; his younger three years after that. Simeon lived through Herod's consolidation of his power and the start of his building campaign in Jerusalem with the theatre, amphitheatre and hippodrome. To Simeon's great sorrow his wife died soon after these events and he retired to a room in the backstreets below the temple mount.

From there he witnessed the building of Herod's great temple.

He knew many of the priests who were retrained to serve as carpenters and masons on the holy site of the shrine itself. He saw the carts with their burdens of stone labouring up the slope. He watched as the huge foundation blocks were eased into place to enlarge the temple site. He saw the dust rise as the walls of the old temple were removed and the new walls rise with their gleaming marble slabs. He met the workmen in the market where he still kept a small table. He sold new

garments to the builders and stitched those that
became torn in the building. He was astonished to
see the shrine go up in just two years and work
mostly completed on the surrounding buildings six
years later. Herod was clearly as energetic as he
was determined. In the evenings Simeon would
walk near the site and marvel as the setting sun
brought fire to the white marble and gold plate.

But Herod's own fire seemed now to subside and
rumours abounded of his domestic troubles which
became openly known with the strangling of his
two sons Alexander and Aristobulus at Samaria
during Simeon's 67th year. Jerusalem lived in fear
as Herod's cruelty increased with his ageing and
infirmity.

And all this time Simeon was waiting.

***

Simeon's waiting was not passive; he was very busy
with his own preparations for the Lord's Anointed.
He regularly attended the temple prayers, making it
his business to attend the morning sacrifice at the
third hour. Occasionally he would also attend the
prayer which accompanied the evening sacrifice at
the ninth hour. At first he would stand as the
scriptures were read, but then, in his old age, he
allowed himself to sit. He took very seriously the
keeping of the commandments; his business was

conducted scrupulously and his daughters brought up in the fear of the Lord.

As Jerusalem was shaken by events political and military, economic and social, the longing grew in his heart for that time when she would be redeemed out of all her troubles. He saw his own devotion as a small contribution to the fulfilment of this great hope; his presence in the city as a daily confirmation that the Saviour would come soon. The building of Herod's temple fuelled his anticipation. Surely this magnificent structure would provide a fitting place to welcome the king! His sense of expectation received confirmation in a most unusual incident in his 68th year.

To say that Simeon often sensed the Spirit of God move upon him in the years after he heard the voice would be wrong. There were occasions when he was particularly moved in prayer or as he heard the scriptures read but on this day he felt nothing unusual as he mounted the temple steps for the ninth hour of prayer. The people congregated as usual and as usual the sacrifice was offered. That which was unusual occurred during the offering of the incense.

The priest who was to offer, entered the shrine to perform the ritual and, as the incense rose, so did the prayers of the people standing outside in the temple courts. The people then waited for the priest

to emerge and give the blessing. They waited and
waited but the man did not appear. Some of the
other priests began to shuffle and murmur to one
another as the prayers of the people ended and the
expected blessing did not occur. The people
murmured also and began looking for some signal
from the priests. They however were at a complete
loss and none dared enter the shrine; only one of
the chief priests would be permitted to investigate.
In the event, shortly after a chief priest had been
sent for, the man emerged from the shrine to give
the blessing but appeared to be unable to do so. He
motioned with his hands and made signs to the
people. Some thought he had had a seizure, others
that he had seen a vision. Another priest spoke the
blessing and the people were dismissed but all were
perplexed by this strange happening. Simeon
questioned his friends among the priests but was
unable to find out much more, though word had it
that it was not a seizure but some sort of vision.

For many days after that, Simeon gazed into his
evening fire and pondered what this might mean.
He was convinced that it concerned the Messiah and
it rekindled hope within him. He would see the
Saviour soon. Yet even as he delighted in the
thought he questioned the circumstances that
surrounded him. Was Israel ready for its Messiah?

***

"It will be a full salvation! You talk, like so many in Israel today, of the restoration of the kingdom and our freedom from foreign rule, but it will be greater than that."

"What do you mean then by 'full'? Are you saying that he will be Messiah of the Greeks and Romans too?"

"Listen!" Simeon was in full flow now. He stood on the edge of the small group of scholars in the portico but now he was the centre of their attention. "Israel was saved out of captivity by Moses who brought our fathers out of Egypt. The Messiah will be greater even than Moses; he will lead an Exodus of all peoples out of the bondage that Adam, the father of all peoples, has led us into. Adam sinned, the Messiah will save all peoples from that captivity to sin."

"No! The Messiah is of the Jews and for the Jews. He is the Son of David. As David defeated the Philistines and extended the boundaries of our nation so his Son will defeat our enemies and make our nation great again."

"What then do you make of Isaiah when he says, 'I will also make you a light for the Gentiles, that you may bring my salvation to the ends of the earth'? Will this not be a full salvation corresponding to the full extent of the world?"

"The Gentiles will be saved only by becoming part of Israel. They will accept the Messiah as universal king. They will accept the covenant of circumcision and become proselytes. They will join Israel. That is how they will be saved!"

"But one becomes a Jew by being circumcised...how then, I ask myself, will light come to those who remain uncircumcised...who stay as Gentiles? For Isaiah speaks of a light to the Gentiles."

"Simeon, how can they receive light and remain unchanged? The light will shine upon the Gentiles and they will desire Torah, they will desire fellowship. Only through entering God's covenant with Abraham will the Gentiles be saved. Only by being circumcised will they be admitted into the light God shines on them through the Messiah. He will trample our enemies and exalt our nation. He will bring glory to Israel."

"But what is the glory of a people Mattan? Is it might? Is it power? Is it control of their own land or the fear and respect of the other nations? The Romans have much of this, are they glorious! What is it then? Is it their education, their culture, their artistry, their temples, statues, libraries? The Greeks have much of this – are they glorious? We in Israel have a different glory. The presence of the Lord among his people. When Moses dedicated the Tabernacle, when Solomon dedicated the temple the light of the glory of the Lord was seen. That was Israel's glory. Blessed is the nation whose God is the Lord!"

"Simeon, Simeon. Do you not see a great new temple even now being built before your eyes – bigger and better even than that of Solomon – this is

Israel's glory. When it is dedicated will not God come in glory again to consecrate it?"

"Will he Mattan? Apart from the sheer grace and mercy of the Almighty was it not because of Israel's purity at that time that He permitted the Tabernacle and temple to be built? Was it not because of the faith of its leaders?"

"Is not the Almighty allowing this magnificent temple to be built today? Perhaps you think too little of the nation's obedience Simeon...or of the grace of God."

"I think of the obedience of Moses the servant of the Lord. I think of David a man after God's own heart. I think of the wisdom of Solomon. These are the foundations for the Lord's living among His people. And why did Ezekiel see the glory depart from the temple? Was it not because of the people's sin and idolatry? Herod indeed is raising a great building here...but will the Lord choose to inhabit it in glory? Who is the Moses, the David or the Solomon of today? Is it Herod?"

"We all know that Herod is Rome's king Simeon. But he has brought peace, as David did. He has shown respect to us Pharisees and God has raised him up at this time to make the temple glorious. I say to you, 'Watch!' As the temple is built the people will consecrate themselves and God will once again dwell in his sanctuary in glory."

"I simply ask, Mattan, whether we as a nation are ready for God's glory. If he were to come to His temple today would he find us more obedient to His commands than were Ezekiel's generation who caused Him to leave?"

***

But Simeon knew that Israel was not ready.

As he sat by his fire in the winter evenings he pondered how it would be for the Messiah when he came. If God's chosen one were to come to Israel today would he be welcomed by the leaders? Would Herod or his dynasty move aside for him to be crowned? Would a Caesar bow at his coronation? Simeon knew the answer. There would be struggle, no-one would move aside without a fight.

But then, who could win against the Lord and His Anointed? No man surely! Simeon was confident of this. What he did not understand though were references in the Scriptures to the Messiah suffering. How could this happen? God suffered when His people were in Egypt, this he knew: 'In all their afflictions I was afflicted.' But was He also afflicted by their slavery to sin now? Or was He rather affronted that they should choose to sin? Helpless slavery or deliberate choice? Where was the boundary that might show where God's wrath ends and his compassion begins? If the Lord did suffer through His people's helpless bondage to sin, then surely His Messiah would also suffer. But then...what was the Lord to do about this?

Behold this child is destined for the falling and rising again of many in Israel
Simeon often found his mind in a whirl with such thoughts. Of one thing he was certain. If he was confused so would most other people be. Many would find their values and their simple ideas about the King greatly challenged by His actual arrival. Many of these ideas, along with the people who held them, would come crashing to the ground. Simeon's hope was that, from the dust of such destruction, correct ideas would rise and with them many who would hold tightly to them.

He will be a sign that is spoken against
Simeon knew that the Messiah would be a highly controversial figure. Just as the people of Israel had so often spoken against Moses and the prophets so they would surely speak against the Messiah. But if he came straightway as a conquering king would there be time for controversy? Wouldn't He just silence every lying tongue and remove every false argument? But then again Isaiah had said he would be despised and rejected by men. There it was, suffering again. Simeon could not make head nor tail of it.

A sword will pierce your own heart too -

As he mended other people's cloaks and cleaned up other people's mess in the streets, Simeon occasionally thought of his own 'walk with God'. He had come to Jerusalem to welcome the king. He had to admit that there were times when he had hoped to make his fortune in Jerusalem. He had wanted to become a wealthy merchant who would honour the arrival of the king by providing a rich welcome for him. He would become one of those great men who entertained the king lavishly and, in so doing, would become one of his intimate friends and confidents. The Lord seemed to go out against his schemes though for all his attempts had failed and here he was scratching about to make a living, reduced to poverty. What sort of welcome could he give the king?

In his more sane moments he knew that he could never out-give God and that the greatest gift he could offer the Messiah was a loving, appreciative and obedient heart. But he had cherished such ideas of what he would do for the king and now had to accept that they would never be fulfilled. That hurt. It was as though the passing years had driven a knife of frustration into that body of dreams which now lay writhing on the ground in the final throes of death. Even now, at times, Simeon felt like screaming and railing against what he saw in such moments as the injustice of it all. At other times he felt like weeping on the floor over the pieces of shattered hopes. Sometimes he did just that. This

Messiah, he had turned his life upside down! There
were times when he wondered if he was still
standing.

*In order that the thoughts of many hearts will be
revealed.*
Why? Why all this frustration? Why all the broken
dreams? They were not all bad, surely! Was he all
bad then? When Simeon's thoughts took this turn
he often used to take a stick and stab at the fire
making the sparks fly upwards. He wasn't all bad!
He had left his home and village his family and
livelihood to await the arrival of the King. He had
kept an honest business. He had not defrauded
anyone. He gave charity. Was he not serving the
King simply by being here in Jerusalem? When
those sparks flew and flames darted out from amid
the tinder they lit up the dark corners of his room
and cast strange shadows on the walls. So also,
when Simeon thought like this the very flames of his
anger seemed to light up the dark recesses of his
own soul revealing fears, worries, prides and
arrogances he was only half aware of at most times
and would hardly admit to at others.

Here he was proudly waiting for the King yet
realising only too well his need for a saviour, one
who would climb down to his ledge, release him
from the things that bound him and hoist him to
safety. The Messiah, when he comes, will be like a
refining fire, purifying the Sons of Levi, but Simeon

knew that it was not only the priests who would need cleansing. Had not Jeremiah the prophet been right when he said, 'the heart is deceitful above all things, and beyond cure. Who can understand it? I the Lord search the heart and examine the mind to reward a man according to his conduct, according to what his deeds deserve'? Simeon stabbed at the fire when his own heart came under scrutiny but the resulting flame only revealed further his own crying need. If the Messiah should come and search the hearts of men, there will surely be those who will stab out at him in wild defence of the darkness within them they are trying to hide.

***

Simeon was now an old man. He shuffled about his small business with the growing awareness that his long wait would soon be at an end. Sometimes he wondered if perhaps the voice, far off now, in his youth and in the southern wastes, had been the imaginings of his own heart. The Messiah would come, He must come for the Scriptures had promised it. Perhaps though he would come later when Simeon's body had found rest in a simple burial.

There were times he longed for that peace. He was in his 70th year. He was far more tired these days. He was not as stable on his feet. His eyesight was still good, and for this he was grateful; with it he was still able to make and mend clothes. But his hearing had become worse recently and there were times when he felt so restless.

Then there was that incident this morning, and Sarah's question. How did he know that the Messiah will come soon? The simple answer was that the Lord had told him he would live to see the Messiah and now he knew he had little time left to live. If God had spoken those years ago then it must be soon.

Simeon put down the bowl, stirred the small fire and reached for some more twigs; a little more heat before he began cutting the new piece of cloth. He became uneasy though; the cloth faded from his mind. He stood up and shuffled to and fro across the small room. Again the great longing enveloped his soul. The Messiah! The Messiah! He stood facing the wall head in his hands. He felt suddenly entombed in his little room and longed for fresh air and light. Out in the alley he turned up the hill for the second time that day, towards the temple.

He entered its precincts. The temple was its usual bustling self with worshippers, visitors and priests, mingling with guards, tradesmen and builders. He walked across the outer court, up the fourteen steps onto the terrace surrounding the inner court and through the Gate of Offering covered with silver and gold, slowly ascending the five steps, into the Court of Israel the most holy ground that he was permitted to tread. Normally, simply being here seemed to restore balance, hope, life. But now the longing continued unfulfilled. He turned towards the spacious Court of the Gentiles to retrace his steps back to his room. A heaviness seemed to enfold him. He could not go, not yet, he must stay here close to the holiest place on earth and bear the longing of his soul once again. He decided to walk slowly around the rampart which separated him from the Court of the Priests, the altar and the Holy of Holies. He shuffled towards his left and turned right behind the shrine. Right again down the north side of the shrine and right again to take him in front of the altar whose smoke could be seen rising over the rampart. For a moment he stood and looked.

Two men passed by him; one was a priest, the other carried two pigeons. He watched as they approached the Priest's Court to offer the sacrifices. The man would lay his hands upon the birds before the priest sacrificed them. He watched as the man waited for the priest to come out and then as the man went through the large gate that led into the women's court. He followed him, though he did not know why. Strange, he had hardly ever entered the women's court; he had no need since his wife had died. He went through the gateway and picked his way carefully down the fifteen steps into the women's area. He saw the man join a young woman and talk with her; she held a bundle in her arms, a baby. Probably the man had just offered the prescribed sacrifices as he presented his firstborn son to the Lord. Some sacrifice! Two young pigeons, the cheapest offering you could buy. He examined the couple more closely; they looked poor, almost destitute.

As he looked, he found he could not take his eyes off them. Why not? He felt drawn towards them and, as he shuffled to where they were, a presence, like a warm coat enveloped him. His muscles became both limp to himself yet enervated at the same time. It was as though he was carried towards the couple and to the bundle in the woman's arms. He became oblivious to all others and began to see only them...him. 'What was happening to him?' he wondered, 'Why this attention? Why this focus? Why this child?' Simeon took a sudden deep breath as the realisation impacted him. His heart beat faster, furious now. The couple moved off; he chased them across the court catching them before they reached the Gate Beautiful. He took the man by the arm and halted him, drawing him to one side. He stared briefly at the mother who looked quizzically at him and then at her husband.

The woman offered the bundle to him. He took the baby from his mother and held him in his arms. Tears began to course down his cheeks as with great tenderness and reverence he brought the child to his own breast. For several moments he hugged the baby closely yet lightly, his muscles, his whole body strangely limp both with that enveloping 'coat' and with the emotion. His head swam as he touched the little one's head and looked into his eyes. No words came and he just stood there, tears in his eyes, looking from one parent to the other and back to the child, swaying gently. The man and woman stood amazed at him and yet something in their gaze showed a lack of surprise almost as though surprises had become the usual with this baby. Their look was all the confirmation he needed. Through eyes swimming with tears he looked upwards and as he found peace the words tumbled out of him one last time.

"According to your word you release your servant in peace
Because my eyes have seen your salvation
Which you have prepared in front of all people
A light for revelation to the Gentiles
And the glory of your people Israel."

He had waited so long, all his life it seemed, for this one moment. Now he not only beheld the Messiah, he actually held him…in his own arms.

As the intensity of the release and joy subsided he knew he had to pass on wisdom from his long walk, particularly to the mother. There she was, beautiful and innocent with the fullness of love and pride in her eyes for her child. He must give her a warning. She must know, if she did not already, that her exalted position carried with it an echo of the pain of the Almighty for his people.

"Understand; this boy is destined to cause many in Israel to fall and rise again.
He is destined to be a sign that men will speak against,
Hence a sword will pierce your soul too.
For through him the thoughts of many people's hearts will be revealed."

He knew he had to pass on something of the wisdom gained through the years of his walk with the Messiah. She could see his joy, but she must be prepared for the inevitable sword. All the beauty of her evident love would be challenged to its foundations by the opposition aroused through this child. Even as he looked into her eyes, though, he could see a nod of acceptance. Of course, as his mother, she had probably had some experience of that sword already.

Simeon returned his gaze to the child and loved him again. There had been many times when he had completed a garment or a particularly difficult mend for a customer. Handing the completed article back, knowing that the job had been done well, had always brought a measure of relief. Now that sense flooded him again as he handed the baby

back to its mother and prepared to take his leave.
Just then, however, the aged widow Anna joined
them. He knew Anna, knew her heart for the
redemption of Jerusalem; he also knew that she had
seen his action and understood its significance. She
would have much on her heart about this child. For
a moment, he and Anna gazed at the couple and
baby, but then Simeon shuffled away to give her the
privacy he himself had enjoyed with the parents.
He would meet her in the temple again and would
have opportunity to talk with her then. For now he
must be home.

The old man shuffled down the hill and into the
backstreets to his room. He lit the fire and ate a
little gruel and dried bread then stared into the
embers and thought. He thought of his goats, of his
move to Jerusalem, of his wedding day and the
births of his daughters. He thought of the
harrowing events when Herod and the Romans
stormed Jerusalem. He then thought of the
magnificence of the temple Herod had built. He
thought of the long years of waiting and delighted
again and again in the recollection of the baby he'd
seen in the temple that day.

No more cloth today, today was a day for thought
and quiet celebration. That evening he walked
through the temple courts again, and again
marvelled at the sunset on the gold and marble.
Hoping for a word with Anna he strolled through

the women's court but she was not to be seen; Ah well, for that he would just have to wait. As he lay down on his pallet that night there was an overwhelming sense of his life's work completed.

***

Simeon's lifeless body was found by his neighbour the next day.

The expression fixed upon his face was that of supreme peace.

5. Three Pillars of Wisdom

It is with a heavy heart and great sadness that I lift the pen this evening. My heart is overwhelmed with the loss of my dear friend Balthazar whose passing into eternity earlier today has left such a void in my life. Raise the pen I must, however, if only to ease the burden of my own soul and to seek that peace I saw in his eyes before they closed for the last time. My heart is heavy within me, yet a resolve is there too for the adventure of strange providence that bound us three as one must be placed on record; though I wonder, even now, how many will believe should they ever read this chronicle.

Let me first recount our lineage, for that must assert its right to defend us against the accusations of insanity which have plagued our lives since then. All three of us are, or I should say were, descended from generations of the wise. We are from noble families bearing the responsibility of preserving the wisdom of the ancients that future generations should not plunge into the awful chaos of ignorance. It is true that the cities to which we ourselves gave our knowledge are not as renowned as they once were, but it is also true that our ancestors served in the capitals of the splendid empires of Babylon and Persia. Oh there are numerous paths of wisdom, many of which are only so-called, and I know that my ancestors have delved into darker secrets that have robbed them of their light and balance, but neither Balthazar, Gaspar nor I can be accused of following such paths. From early times we have been trained in the highly respected schools of wisdom in Ancient Persia and have followed the oracles of, among others, Balaam of Pethor, Belteshazzar of Babylon and Jeremias of Jerusalem. We have enjoyed the privileges of wisdom drawn from as far away as Egypt on the Nile to the peoples of the Indus, all with a leavening of soundness drawn from the small Jewish communities within our midst. I shall maintain to my death couch that we are not fools given to vanities. That would be to betray our illustrious heritage. Yet I do admit to our engaging upon a peculiar expedition, the account of which, with the passing of Balthazar, I feel burdened now to write down.

For all three of us the journey began, not with the first step of our camels but years before, with those perambulations of the mind which were fuelled by our studies as young men. We were passing through a course of lectures on prophecies drawn mainly from the Jewish scriptures of that period they referred to as their 'exile'. I have to admit that for us this so called 'exile' was a boon of untold richness, for, when Nebuchadnezzar of Babylon conquered their small state beside the western sea, he uncovered a spring of wisdom so strong and pure that, when it flowed into Babylon with the captives, it so transformed the fetid waters of the wisdom then prevailing as to render it sweet and vital. All three of us found these lectures invigorating and highly stimulating and it was from these studies that we first understood of the birth of the great king.

What appealed to us most was the recognition that this King of the Jews, the one they called their 'Messiah', might actually appear in our own lifetimes. Let me explain in straightforward fashion. To Belteshazzar of Babylon it had been revealed by the Divine Being whom Nebuchadnezzar himself had called the 'God of gods' that a certain number of 'weeks' of years would pass from that time until this great king would appear. We were told that this king would suffer a violent end yet 'not for himself', a phrase that absorbed and perplexed us. From our own calculations at that time, we understood that his significant passage into the world of the dead would occur some fifty years hence. We reasoned rather simply then that if his death were fifty years away and if he were a respected elder by then, say around fifty years old, well, that his birth was imminent. We enthused, even as we studied these things, that he might already be born. So wild did we become that we even accosted travellers from the west for information of a new king in Jerusalem, but there was no such news.

Other magi of course disagreed with our surmisings and reasons, arguing that no wisdom could or even would be that accurate. They retorted that these words were figures, parables, riddles; that a straightforward reading was superficial and evaded the deeper wisdom. Such even was the view of our old school lecturer. Our response had been to refer them to the historical accuracy of much of Belteshazzar's prophecies and to the historical context of Balaam's proclamations. We argued that these prophecies, rooted in history, would have historical fulfilment in the lives of men. Our critics agreed in general, but rejected our 'crude literalism' as they put it. For a while the dispute had excited interest among the magi of our city and some had joined our 'little school' as it was called. As the years passed though, the excitement subsided, our group dwindled and the dribblings of news from the west brought nothing significant. I fear that our small group was written off as of marginal interest by the majority. That we were also becoming an object of humour was confirmed as events unfolded.

Unable to convince others of our excited expectations and finding ourselves both subject to ridicule and embarrassment, we tended to withdraw into our own group. This, sadly, merely reinforced our isolation and created an internment from which we found it increasingly hard to find release. As our excitement grew, so did our estrangement from the main body of Parthian magi and our own frustration with their deaf ears and latent sneers. Quietly then we read and discussed and examined again the ancient writings which fuelled our fascination.

Balaam in his oracle had spoken of Jacob's powerful ruler who would inflict judgement upon Moab, the very nation who had hired him to curse Jacob's descendants. What began to intrigue us was the portent that would herald this ruler's arrival. Our disputations focussed upon these words:

"A star will come out of Jacob;
A sceptre will rise out of Israel."

Some of our members, myself included, maintained that this indicated that the ruler's arrival would be announced by a planetary conjunction or some glorious new star in the heavens. Others among us hotly disagreed and retorted that the second line explained the first and that the 'star' was simply another phrase for 'sceptre', just as 'Israel' was another name for 'Jacob'. Their argument had much in its favour in both the rhythm of the poetry and the explanatory sense of the oracle, however a few of us remained persuaded that a literal star would arise in the west from the direction of the empire of the Romans.

Years passed and with them the urgency of the debate. If the king was to die violently at, say, fifty, as a respected elder in Judea, he would already be a boy, even a young man in his early teens. We would then have missed his nativity and our persuasion about a literal star would have been misguided. What kept waning hope alive with the passing of those years was the possibility that the king might be 'cut off' as a younger man, say aged forty-five, or forty, thirty-nine, thirty-eight, thirty-seven – our counting I confess was becoming desperate and more of our small number were persuaded against our 'absurd dream' as they put it.

We began to feel ourselves clutching at straws in the wind as, night after night, we examined the western horizon for the longed for appearance. Many others, of course, each for their own reasons, studied the constellations and movements, hoping thereby, some of them, to predict their own or another's future. Some showed interest in our search and speculated how such an appearance might affect their prosperity or security. But our intense focus on the western sky was condemned as narrow minded by many and more than once we were referred to as the 'Owls of Susa' for our nocturnal exertions.

Night after night, nothing. Month in, month out, even the Moon's steady, predictable circling began to challenge our hope. It seemed so stable, so clear, so regular when our flighty star had not even shown its face. The years passed towards absurdity, thirty-

seven, thirty-six, thirty-five. Surely, if we were right
the king would have been born a decade since. I
have to confess that my own night surveyings
waned in interest. Other ideas became a focus of
attentions and the star of less personal significance.
Surely the king, if Belteshazzar could be trusted,
had already been born. Perhaps then our star, if
there was to be one, would indicate his accession to
the throne. If so it could put the star's appearance a
decade hence. In truth though, our excitement had
dwindled; our hope was disappearing like water
into desert sands.

Then came that glorious night when all was
transformed!

I had retired to my couch after an exhausting day
spent delving in the library. A heavily clouded sky
gave no promise of stargazing and I was weary.
About midnight I had become restless in my sleep
and had finally roused myself to call for medicinal
wine to secure sleep before the business of the
following day. As I waited for my slave to appear
my drowsiness suddenly fled as I noticed a beautiful
light steady upon the opposite wall. Accustomed as
I was to the full moonlight behind me this was
strange. I shifted in my couch and looked out into a
clear night. In a moment I was out and onto the
balcony. The light emitted from a star of rare
beauty that had arisen. I took my bearings; indeed
it has arisen over the western horizon. For a

moment I gazed at its quiet light streaming not only full into my face but seeming to bathe me in its radiance, beginning to fill my soul with a half-forgotten excitement and nervous anticipation.

I left my drugged wine and instead ordered my slave to fetch a light and a night watchman. I would go immediately to my colleagues and wake them. Too late! A knock at my own door told me they had been first to see the star. Three of us gathered again on my balcony and the silver light fuelled our conversation and group spirit. Instantly we agreed that this must be the star for which we had waited some fifteen years and more. The question now became, "What of our response?" What should we do now that the star had arrived? Strangely, in all our deliberations, we had never addressed this point. As we stood there however, the three of us bathed in this glorious light, our spirits were lifted to that 'God of gods' and our hearts were filled with gratitude. It was in those moments that the urge to worship that God was born in us. We stood, as it were on a mountain peak of inspiration, the culmination of years of discussion, of study and of waiting and the night sky above us seemed filled with the light of this magnificent star. It was almost calling us, upward, to be uprooted from this earth. It called us to soar into the heavenlies where it itself was at home. It called us westwards to where it was born, arising from the birth, yes the birth of the king whose magnificence it portrayed. We agreed that we must make preparations for a journey to Judea, to worship the king. From that moment our conversation was animated with notes of preparation, means of travel, the number of slaves – if any, the distances and times, provisions and protection and yes...the gifts we should bring as tokens of our homage. What gifts would befit the king from heaven who would die violently 'but not for himself'?

It was late into the night by the time I retired to bed, even then sleep eluded me and I drifted tired into the new day.

The thrill of our small group however received amazing and perplexing rebuff as soon as we began to share our news.

There had been others observing last night but none had seen an unusual star in the west!

We urged them to watch again the next night and watch they did, in their hundreds I believe, as we did also, but stranger still the star could not be found. I was baffled, deflated and exhausted the following morning. Not only was our own disappointment great but the jeers of our colleagues was unbearable. Our tiny group tightened into resolve as the pressure upon us increased. We had seen the star! We were not deluded. It was there, where expected, even if it had challenged our ideas of when.

Our preparations to travel west, though slow, were spurred on by the crescendo of mockery that greeted our every visible move to ready ourselves. A further, more sinister move hastened our desire to leave. It was clear that we were going west to greet the birth of a new king. Our own kingdom, however was in the empire of the Parthians, whereas Judea was in that of Rome; the two empires had been enemies for fifty years or more. Only recently had a 'balance of power' been tacitly agreed with the return of Crassus' captured eagles. Our move towards Rome and a 'Roman' king was, in some quarters, mooted as treason. We were relieved indeed that any such accusations amounted only to words. Perhaps in a strange way the ridicule that we endured was itself a shield to a far more dangerous threat.

To many, we were just harmless buffoons and our colleagues were too busy laughing at us to take any treason seriously. We sought and, eventually, received official permission for our journey, yet, after it had begun, our hearts tilted on a knife edge as we expected any minute to hear a thunder of cavalry hooves, the herald of a detachment assigned to escort us back home, even to stand trial. Crossing the border itself was fraught with tension as we passed out of Parthia into Roman territory, but thereafter we journeyed more easily unburdened from the threatened accusations of disloyalty.

And journey we did. Crossing the Tigris we passed
the ruins of old Babylon's grandeur where our
'teacher' Belteshazzar had lived for so long before
being assigned to our own city of Susa. Moving
north along the east bank of the great Euphrates, we
traced the well-worn caravan path around the great
and dreadful desert to the west.   Eventually we
crossed the river and proceeded due west with the
desert to the south of us. It was then that we came
under Roman dominion, as our encounter with the
formal and ordered outposts informed us. Money
had to be changed, business declared and warrants
issued.

Ours was an easy excuse; we were travelling wise
men, sophists they called us, on our way to the city
of Jerusalem and thence to the library in Alexandria.
Nothing was mentioned of the gold we carried
though. The three of us had travelled
inconspicuously betraying nothing of our wealth,
standing or purpose. The guard let us through with
a bemused frown; Jerusalem, why Jerusalem? It
was not a pilgrimage month!

But for us it could only be Jerusalem. Where else
was the king to be born but in the capital of Judea?
And so on towards that renowned city we travelled.
South-westwards to the Nabataean city of
Damascus and then skirting the snow-capped
heights of Mount Hermon we plunged down into the

luxuriant warmth of the Jordan valley. Following the shores of Genessaret our beasts plodded the famous 'Way of the Sea' along the Jordan to the town of Jericho where we were advised to join another group that was apprehensively waiting to swell its numbers before embarking upon the final, inhospitable, barren and dangerous stadia to Jerusalem.

One could recount in detail aspects of our journey, the exertions and exhaustions, the fears of robbery which swelled again as we wound up the hills beyond Jericho, the outrageous prices of inns along our way, but it is sufficient to say that when our eyes beheld Jerusalem the toil was washed away amid tears of joy. We had arrived...or so we thought!

For it is now that this account takes a most curious and ominous turn.

Taking rooms in an expensive residence and now displaying our previously concealed finery we sought and were granted, I think because of our appearance, an audience with the king, Herod by name. His court was rather austere by our eastern standards but the elderly gentleman was gracious in his reception of us. Our business he had already heard in part, but he was generous in the time he gave us and asked, intelligently, many questions.

To our question about the royal child, though, he
could not reply. No royalty had born male children
in Jerusalem for several years and certainly none
since our star had appeared. To us of course this
was a great shock and most unhappy news. We had
fed for months upon the sighting of the star; that
one sighting had surmounted our years of waiting
to fuel us through much ridicule, doubt and toil
along our way. But this clear refutation of royal
birth alarmed and deeply saddened us. Herod, I
believe, perceived this and questioned us further.
We explained that it was the great king of the Jews
we sought and said again that we had seen the
rising of his star in the east and had come to
worship him. I felt this last affirmation unnerved
the king somewhat. Certainly he dismissed us soon
afterwards saying that he would take counsel and
grant us a second audience. We were of course very
grateful and took the gentleman's distraction to be
an indication of his compassion upon our
frustration. In that moment we grasped the king's
generous sympathy...and missed entirely the
ominous motive that was later to be revealed.

We should have been alerted for Herod, we learned,
was not himself a Jew and of course might feel
threatened by the nativity of a pure Jewish king.
But our minds, for all their wisdom, were dulled.
We hardly noticed the secrecy of our next audience,
so eager were we to have some news to cast light
upon our quest. But, recalling it now, it was in

secret that Herod met us, and there conveyed the wisdom of the Jewish seers and scholars. Amongst all our books in the east were many Jewish texts, but not all it transpired. Clearly none of us had encountered the book of Micah, another prophet it seems. The book must have been absent from the shelves of our libraries or had been overlooked in our studies. Apparently though it was this oracle which foretold the birthplace of the king whom the Jews referred to as the Messiah, as Belteshazzar himself had done. According to this book the Messiah was not to be born in Jerusalem at all. For all our learned wisdom, we were still uninformed. The king was to be born in a place a few stadia to the south; a small town by the name of Bethlehem.

King Herod had been most generous in clarifying our quest. We still had no misgivings when he gave us a personal commission. He intimated to us that our strange adventure both fascinated and delighted him. He asked us, in return for his trouble, merely to inform him when we locate the child so that he too would be in a position to quietly lower his own crown in homage to the king. We were delighted at this suggestion of a fellow pilgrim and agreed of course. We left his presence most uplifted. After all the months of ridicule and scorn we had won a king to our cause; a most worthy ally indeed, for we would then enjoy his protection.

We did not notice the apprehensive stares of the people in the streets or the worried look on our innkeeper's face. We were not from Jerusalem and had by now become accustomed to eyes following us with myriad thoughts and impressions behind them. The truth, we discovered later, was that the city was perturbed by our visit. Better than we, they knew their old king. For all our wisdom we left Jerusalem blissfully unaware that our generous benefactor and convert was a gruesome tyrant bathed in the blood of even his own sons. As heralds of a new king, we were, to the people of Jerusalem, portents of another wave of bloody purging. It may have been that many were relieved to see us turn out of the city gates and towards the south that evening, for, where we would go, there the awful axe would fall. As I say though, of all this we had no idea. In our innocence and simplicity we were eager to go on to Bethlehem, there to look for the child.

Hardly had we left Jerusalem though, than we were faced with a dilemma. Behind us was the capital with the palace as its royal centre. Before us was an unknown town with no obvious place for the birth of a king. How then were we to find him? By now we had another clue for the name of an ancient king, David, had been supplied by Herod. The child was, we understood, to be a descendant of his. Perhaps then the boy had recently been born to some family whose lineage went back to that king. Perhaps there would be a family house, a mansion of faded splendour in which the baby even now lay. Certainly we would have to enquire and, as Herod had said, search diligently for the child.

But as we discussed the problem the possible ramifications seemed endless and the gathering darkness seemed to cast shadow after shadow upon our way. What were we to do? Were we to enter the first house and pay homage to the first male child we encountered? How were we to enquire? Would a register of births be kept in the town? We imagined ourselves entering house after house requesting audience with a king whose birth no one in Jerusalem had heard of. What retorts would greet us? What further ridicule would we have to endure? What inane fellows we might seem to be to the populace of Bethlehem? We imagined a crowd of children begging for our shekels as we knocked upon another door. We imagined them gathering round and mocking our quest, making us look utter fools by dressing one of their fellows in a silly crown and ushering us solemnly into his presence before bursting into hysterical laughter. The practicalities of the search in Bethlehem loomed larger with every step of our plodding beasts.

How were we to find an unknown baby king in that town?

Then it was that it happened!

Having descended into the valley of Gehenna or Ben
Hinnom as they also call it, discussing our problem
all the way, we ascended onto the plain that
stretched southwards So busy were we with our
problem that we did not notice it at first, but the
clouds had silently parted to reveal a clear night sky
lit with myriad stars; and there, gleaming like the
prize jewel in a crown was the star we had seen in
the east. We had not expected it. For months we
had not seen it; as quickly as it had appeared to us
that one night in Susa so quickly it had disappeared
again.

Now, to our amazement and wonder it had
reappeared as if to shed light on the very problem
we faced. We immediately dismounted and,
cavorting like silly boys in a stream, we bathed
again in its magnificent light. We were absolutely
thrilled and took hold of each other in great relief
and joy. The heavy burden of doubt that had
haunted each of us since the star had disappeared,
the weeks of torment each of us had bottled up in
his heart now burst out in glorious relief. We
danced like madmen.

As, gradually, sense returned and we mounted the
camels for the final leg of our journey, the star,
whose appearance had been so incredibly timely,
now seemed to perform an even stranger act. Of
course we could not take our eyes off of it and left

the camels to find their own footholds on the well-worn path. As we gazed though, we gradually became aware that the star appeared to change position. It was high in the night sky but seemed to be passing other stars... moving.

Several times we drew near to one another and remarked upon this phenomenon in voices that became increasingly hushed. More clearly now, as we moved so, slowly, did the star. We looked at each other and, in its light, saw perplexity in our fellow's faces. What was going on here? In those moments I can only describe it as though it were linking up with us. It appeared to 'wait' for us and 'move' with us. It was describing an arc that led inexorably southwards, the direction we ourselves were heading.

We knew sufficient elements of astronomy to be astounded at its perambulation through the heavens. It was an amazing astronomical body, quite unlike any we had witnessed before in all our gazing at and mapping of the stars when at school and beyond. We were awed by it. Were it not for our sheer joy in seeing its powerful radiance again we might easily have been terrified, imagining this event to comprise some awful portent. Instead we became quiet and now glanced at it regularly to confirm its course. We felt it almost possessed 'mind' or was itself being moved by some powerful intelligence. Certainly we were silenced in its presence and considered it to be somehow 'leading' us.

Travelling through that unforgettable night, our path lit by its brilliance, we were again astounded that we were alone. We imagined that all the world's astrologers and stargazers would be converging upon Bethlehem, that the roads and paths to the town would be thronged. However, when we reached the houses, we were alone and our camels plodded through deserted streets. Our consternation concerning our search for the king rose within us again. Which of the houses was he in?

Hardly had we begun to discuss this issue again than our amazement at the star reached a still more unbelievable climax. We had been talking with each other and looking at the dim shapes of houses before us when suddenly the shadows began to move rapidly. Our faces swung around as the star appeared to fall from the sky, much to our consternation. I let out a sharp cry so sudden was its descent but in a moment it stood still gleaming over the outline of one particular house.

We were dumbfounded yet knew instantly that our star was even now pinpointing the very house in which the king lay. All sense of astrological reason had now fully departed; this 'star' admitted of personality. We felt as though we were like...like

113

sheep being led by a celestial shepherd or that the star was a servant sent to usher us into the presence of the Messiah. We stood for a while simply gazing at the sight then, padded up to the 'house', such as it was, where I dismounted and began softly to tap on the door. My colleagues were transfixed by the star that had again behaved in a most unusual fashion; it had lifted slightly to a position above the house and now bathed the whole scene in its wonderful radiance.

Even at that late hour the door swung open and we were met with the incredulous stare of a youngish man who drew back slightly from us. As with Herod we spoke in Greek and found ourselves understood and permitted entry. The scene that greeted us was simple in the extreme. A poor fellow and his wife in cheap rented accommodation, sparsely furnished. A crib in one corner beneath a lamp on a ledge and, in his mother's arms, the baby.

The baby! For a moment the very ordinariness of it all seemed to hurl a final mockery at us. Was this what we had believed in for so long? Was this what we had endured the disintegration of our honour for and had travelled so far to see? Where was the finery? Where was the splendour? Where was the brilliance to illuminate the king's arrival? It was then that we looked back into the street and saw it lit by that strange yet powerful light.

Turning again to the child, now in its crude crib, the last resistance of our worldly honour broken by the simplicity of the scene, we first bowed, then knelt, then our heads touched the dust before the babe as we sobbed out our homage. If, with the return of the star, we had danced with joy, now we wept with relief. That which had held us, which had constrained our lives for decades, which had absorbed our thoughts and studies and deliberations, that which had drawn our days to its purpose was now resolved.

All three of us shed tears of release. Behold the king, the king of the Jews, yet our king too, the king of wise men far away. A star had arisen out of Jacob, a light to lighten we non-Jews too. In this babe a sceptre was rising out of Israel; a baby born in squalor, a king accessible then in a way Herod could never be. We had access, a second private 'interview' with royalty in two days. Shaking slightly I lay my gift before the child, opened the lid of the casket and its content, coins of pure gold, glowed warm in the light of the lamp.

If I had understood and held to the significance of the babe as king, Gaspar was awed by another designation; that the child was unique priest. He would represent the people to God and God to the people in an unsurpassable capacity. But as my companion lowered his vessel to the ground and removed the lid another thought filled my mind.

115

Amid the common odours of the hovel a rich aroma of Frankincense arose and I was transported back to the temples of Susa where the priests would offer such to the local gods and I saw Gaspar as a priest offering incense to...to God! I was taken aback for a moment by the impact of this sight and its meaning. Then my mind cleared and I understood, for, who else could have orchestrated the appearance and movement of the star? What Power alone could bend the celestial bodies to His will? Yet how could this child accomplish this and how could God become a man? I did not know.

By this time Balthazar was approaching. His offering was myrrh. We all knew what this signified; that perplexing death he would undergo in later years, 'After sixty-two weeks the Messiah will be cut off, but not for himself'. Our calculations had centred upon this oracle; it was the key which had alerted us to the time of the king's death and, by backward surmising, to the approximate time of his birth.

For years we had lived under the shadow of this mathematic. It had gripped us and wrested from us our dignity among the magi of Susa. We had left our fine homes and luxuries for a pilgrimage that others had despised and scoffed at. At times it seemed as though our minds were being warped by its numbers and in recent days our knowledge had proved incomplete. Only the gracious appearance of

the star had preserved us from humiliation in
Bethlehem. But now, as the pungency of myrrh
invaded the aroma of incense, our own sacrifices
paled beside that which this child would undergo.
But if 'not for himself'...then for whom? I wondered
again.

Balthazar's worship became for me a moment of
revelation; this supreme king and God would die
for...for all...for all things...the whole of creation's
long and bitter groaning would somehow begin its
sigh of relief in his death. Balthazar himself had
known much suffering in his own life. To him this
gift was of high significance and I saw the tears of
release mingle with the dust at his knees.

So we made our prostrations, said our words and
gave our gifts. Our rather formal acts had, it is true,
been graced with moments of insight and
appreciation in which our own thoughts and lives
were furthered, but, shortly after our veneration
was complete our final act of meeting this small and
rather overawed family began; we talked.

The couple understandably enquired of the reason
for our entrance and worship. We naturally gave
details of our studies, our travels, our meeting with
the king and of course the star. At this last mention
the man, Joseph, made a remark which took the
breath from us. As we described how the star had,
to our amazement, fallen from the heavens to

pinpoint this very house, he said, in rather a matter of fact way, "Another angel." The three of us turned to one another mouths agape for this was one idea we had never entertained. We asked him then of 'other angels' and heard remarkable accounts of heavenly messengers visiting both him and his wife, even to a group of herdsmen on the night of the birth. Again we were compromised; instead of we magi, it had been shepherds who had been given the honour of first homage to the Messiah. Outshone by herdsmen! Our humbling, it seemed, was complete!

Once again though events would prove us wrong.

We finally asked the couple concerning their reaction to our homage. So much had turned out contrary to our expectations that we spoke quite freely and innocently. They were amazed of course...yet in recent weeks had become somewhat accustomed to such things. They thanked us for our generous gifts which would be very useful in a practical way in their present desperate circumstances. We asked if, by chance, other magi or astrologers, other star gazers had come to them. We were, by now, not surprised to hear that no-one else had followed the star whose appearing then, it seemed, had been reserved for us. We felt...humbled, honoured and perplexed, but our business was complete and, rather exhausted, we took our leave retiring to the inn to rest. We would return to Jerusalem the next day and greet Herod our benefactor with the news that would so delight him. How glorious, a king to bow before the king of kings!

That was our intention, but it was never fulfilled.

Exhausted from our exertions, we slept much of that day in our rooms at the inn, removing the finery we had donned for our audience with Herod. Following a walk and meal in the late afternoon we slept again intending to go back to the capital at first light. Then it was that the final act of our adventure unexpectedly came to us whilst we were asleep that evening.

For to two of us, in different forms came essentially the same dream. We had on our walk discussed further the remarkable idea that our star had been an angel. In my dream that star appeared again and led us southwards around the Salt Sea and then north to Damascus. Balshazzar dreamed of an angel closing the gates of Jerusalem to us. Finding each other already awake, we knocked on Gaspar's door and, before the end of the first watch, had deliberated together and decided to make our move at once. We secured provisions from the innkeeper, saddled our camels and padded out of Bethlehem's dark streets shortly after the watch was changed.

We were in part dismayed by these perturbing dreams for we longed to share our discovery of the

Messiah with Herod that he might pay homage to the child as he had said, 'in his own way'. We felt as though we were betraying his confidence in us and were repaying him deceit for his protection. Yet the startling dreams were insistent and we merely obeyed concluding that the Almighty might have a better plan for leading Herod to the babe.

So we returned to our own land and to our homes, our libraries and our studies. Our hopes that we might be accorded some little respect from our fellow magi upon the report of our adventure were soon dashed. The 'night owls of Susa' had gone hunting by night it seemed, but had only caught a little mouse! Our protestations availed little and we were reminded that our absence had occasioned much extra work for our fellows. Only a few, really out of politeness we felt, made time to listen to our accounts. The business of state resumed its demands and any thoughts of another journey westwards were subsumed under its weight.

We could never forget our pilgrimage though, and were always eager for news from Jerusalem, Alexandria or Damascus. Thus it was, about a year later, that rumours began to filter through of horrid events that had taken place in a small town south of Jerusalem; something about a massacre of the local population. We enquired of the Jews in the local synagogue in Susa but they knew nothing. About a month after this, however, the synagogue leader

sent a message asking for an interview. We
received him and, after exchanging pleasantries,
understood that he now had firm news concerning
our earlier enquiry. To our dismay he related how,
some months previously, Herod, the tyrannical king
of Judaea, shortly before his own death, had
authorised his soldiery to slaughter all the male
infants in and around Bethlehem. We were aghast
but said nothing for, I think in that moment, that an
awful apprehension had seized each of us.

That evening we met and began to assemble, piece
by piece, a possible scenario. At first I was very
unwilling to believe anything evil of Herod. He had
been our benefactor. He had assured us of his
delight at the birth of the king. He had extended his
protection to us and was one of the few to show
genuine interest in our quest. But to Balshazzar a
completely different picture was emerging. He
began with our two dreams the evening we had left
Bethlehem and argued that our immediate
departure had robbed Herod of information
concerning the child's whereabouts. We were his
contacts and we had deserted him. Then Balshazzar
spoke out what each of us dreaded to think. If
Herod were indeed capable of such atrocity, then
his target in Bethlehem surely was the new king. He
had deceived us about his intentions and we were
responsible for alerting him to the Messiah who for
him then was a rival.

If we had not gone to Jerusalem, the massacre would never have occurred!

The realisation left us shocked and utterly dejected. For a while we were haunted by the spectre that Herod had killed the babe. Once again we bemoaned our lack of understanding. We, wise magi of Susa, had gone to Jerusalem in error and now had no idea whether the person of our veneration had not become the victim of our ignorance. Each of us were reduced as the shock penetrated our very bones. It was several days before wisdom again asserted itself. Two elements lifted us from the despond into which we had fallen. Firstly was the prophecy; if the Messiah was to be cut off 'but not for himself' then such a death would be too significant to be accomplished in secret by some sword in Bethlehem. Surely, we reasoned, it would be a 'high' death, one that, being for the world, would arrest the attention of the world. Secondly those numbers again. Checking our calculations merely assured us that the death was not to happen now but some thirty years hence; the sixty two weeks were not due to be completed until then.

Thus it was that, in the midst of our distress, we derived some small comfort from our studies, calculations and personal experiences. The king, we believed, had somehow escaped. This was a reassurance yet I knew that Balthazar had been

permanently shaken by this news. I talked with him
in later years and knew that he felt keenly the
responsibility of the male children in Bethlehem.
"Our fault! Our fault!" he would say again and again
when we spoke of these things. I drew him back to
our star and argued that if it had led us from
Jerusalem to the house in Bethlehem could it not
have appeared earlier and led us to by-pass the
capital and Herod altogether? His reply was always
the same, "If it was shining after Jerusalem it must
have been shining before but our own self-
importance at the gates of the city blinded us to its
light." For years our discussion reached stalemate
and I watched helplessly as my dear friend
struggled beneath an overwhelming sense of guilt.

We are old men now. Never again were we able to
travel west. Never again has anything so
remarkable happened in our lives. We have been
blessed, I have children and grandchildren of my
own now and even if the other magi of our age smile
at our 'escapade' as they now term it, I see the
wonder in my grandchildren's eyes as I tell of our
journey to the king far away. They can never get
enough of the star, though I fear that it is to them at
times something of a magical fairy tale. Gaspar
stumbles with his stick as we walk together and
Balthazar has been bedridden for some weeks now.
He still bore the weight of guilt to his couch and,
until recently, laboured beneath it.

I am very tired now and see a red glow in the east; I've been writing all night. But I must set down the last piece of the mosaic.

It was last week when Balthazar's servant hurried to me with an urgent summons to attend his master. I went at once to his room and found him as usual upon his couch but in a state of considerable agitation. When the door was closed he almost ordered me to sit and immediately began to retrace episodes from our strange journey. He was at times incoherent but it became clear to me that some new insight had gripped him. He pointed to a scroll beside his couch and, propping himself up on his elbow bade me read it...read it! After a few lines I recognised it as a scroll from the book of Jeremias the Jewish prophet, and continued reading where it had lain open.

"A voice is heard in Ramah,
Mourning and great weeping,
Rachel weeping for her children
And refusing to be comforted
Because her children are no more."

"That is it" he said "that is it!"
I did not understand. I could perceive no reason for his excitement so asked him to explain.
"Who is Rachel?" He asked.
"Jeremias' Rachel would be one of the two wives of the Jewish patriarch Jacob." I replied.

"Yes, yes! And when might she have wept so over her two sons?"

"Because they are no more," I read "because they have died?"

"No, no! She had two boys both of whom outlived her. Don't you remember: Joseph, the elder became a great leader in Egypt and Benjamin, the younger, went to live with him there. She is not weeping because they have died...but because she is dying. She will not see her boys again because she is dying!"

"Oh." I said rather lamely, still no wiser as to his meaning.

"She died giving birth to the younger son."

"I am sorry my friend," I said, "but I do not follow your argument."

"She died mourning and weeping...in Bethlehem!"

"Bethlehem! But..." I began, but he was already in full flow.

"She died near Bethlehem and was buried there! Go to the first book of the Jewish scriptures and you will find it said that she was buried 'on the way to Ephrath, that is Bethlehem. Now recall what we learned from Herod's counsellors about the birth of the Messiah. We secured that scroll years ago. It says 'But you...'

"...Bethlehem Ephrathah" I joined him, "though you are small among the clans of Judah, out of you will come for me one who will be ruler over Israel."

"Exactly" he continued, "Where Jacob's beloved wife was buried, there the Messiah will be born. But just as she wept for her sons there, there also will great weeping surround the king's birth – Jeremias is prophesying about the future. When the Messiah is born near Rachel's grave, her weeping will be echoed by the women of Bethlehem as they mourn the death of their sons."

"So you are saying that Herod's slaughter of those boys was predicted beforehand?"

"My friend, six hundred year ago!"

"Then our visit to Herod was not due to arrogant blindness on our part?"

"No." He was weeping now and I knew that for him the great burden of his guilt was lifting even as through his tears he continued, "No. I have come to accept what you have said all along my friend. The star appeared at the right moment and we did not miss it at all. The mover of the star allowed us to visit Herod in our ignorance. He could have stopped us but he did not; and that for a deeper reason than I understand my friend, than I understand. All I do understand is that Rachel is told to restrain her weeping. Read further in the scroll."

"Restrain your voice from weeping and your eyes from tears," I continued,

"For your work will be rewarded, declares the Lord. They will return from the land of the enemy. So there is hope for your future, declares the Lord."

"Do you know where the land of the enemy might be?" He asked.

"Go on," I said, for I knew by now that I was but the sounding board for his thoughts.

"It might be here. Where the Jews were brought into exile under Nebuchadnezzar. To Babylon and to Susa."

"There are other countries." I said.

"True, but Susa also. Do you know what?" he suddenly continued, "We Gentiles, from the land of the enemy, travelled to Judea to worship the true ruler of Israel. Perhaps, in some way, we confirmed that there is hope for the future of Rachel. She wept again when we went there but there will come a time when the Gentiles will lead her children home and then her weeping will turn to joy."

"When her Messiah comes?" I said.

"When her Messiah comes! He repeated. "And when will he appear?" He asked.

"Our journey was thirty years ago" I replied, "he may even have appeared by now."

"But…" and with this he raised himself still further and caught hold of my arm; his voice shook with emotion as he affirmed, "But he must be cut off…."

"Yes he must be cut off", I agreed, "You yourself gave the myrrh."

"The myrrh, yes, I know." He slumped down upon his couch again. "Herod tried to kill him at his birth. Surely Herod's offspring will try to kill him in his appearing as a man."

"Yes but, if they should succeed in bringing him to a violent end, you and I, and Gaspar, we all know that it will not be for himself."

"No," he agreed, "it will not be for himself, it will be for others. The king of the world will give his life for the world...even for the Gentiles."

For a while we continued discussing the perplexing questions that these conclusions raised, but Balthazar soon became tired and I left him to rest.

This morning we were summoned to his couch again. We talked once more of the journey and of the star but no more of the slaughtered innocents. Balthazar was at peace now. The guilt, that had burdened him these thirty years, had gone. From his own heart it had been transferred to the heart of the Almighty who had foretold through Jeremias hundreds of years ago that this must happen. Within the whole plan of God, the star appeared again at just the right moment. I smiled as I recalled our cavorting outside Jerusalem when we saw it again. But that life which had so animated Balthazar in that moment was, even in this moment, slipping away and Gaspar and I wept again as we said our farewells to our precious companion. He had born the burden of a guilt that belonged to all of us and in his peace we who remained found peace too.

The red of the eastern sky has turned to orange. I am exhausted from taking the pen through the long night. But my account is finished and whoever will, may read it. Above, in the purple, shines a bright star, it is but the Morning Star though - the herald of the new day.

It is not our angel...

...the herald of a still more glorious Day.

6. The Old King

The old king stroked his beard between his thumb and forefingers and mused. As often in such moments, he returned to the milestones of his reign and reflected on the foundations that supported it, the chief of which was...Rome. Antipater, his father, had shown him the way. Firstly, one had to feed Roman avarice with bribes...large bribes. Secondly the current ruler of Rome had always to be shown absolute loyalty. Thirdly one had to do a good job of extending Roman power and keeping the Roman peace. Finally, where possible, one had always to seek the personal friendship of the highest.

Antipater's policy had worked; it had raised him from obscurity to being the right hand man of Hyrcanus the Jewish high priest appointed by the Roman general Pompey nearly sixty years before. Antipater had worked wonders for his family. Content to rest in the shadow of Hyrcanus, he had once saved Julius Caesar's life – and had won rich rewards from that powerful Roman including many privileges for the Jews. On his death, his eldest son, Phasael, had been made governor of Jerusalem and his younger son, Herod, governor of Galilee. The old king smiled. Antony, Caesar's successor, had himself congratulated him on the energy and military brilliance he had shown on Rome's behalf in Galilee.

Then came the Parthian invasion.

The Parthians were Rome's great enemy on her eastern border, just beyond Galilee and Syria. They had stung Rome badly when the wealthy Crassus lost his legions, their eagles and his own life at the Battle of Carrhae fifty years before. Thirteen years later they had invaded Judaea from the north and taken Jerusalem. They mutilated Hyrcanus to prevent his being high priest any longer and took him prisoner to Babylon. Herod's brother, Phasael, had committed suicide and Herod himself only escaped by the skin of his teeth to the fortress of Masada, from which he fled to Rome. Again the old king smiled at the turn of fate; how well this had all turned out for him.

In Rome he had hoped, perhaps, to take after his father and become right hand man to the new high priest Aristobulus. Instead Antony, Octavian and the Senate set aside the Jewish Hasmonean dynasty and had made himself, Herod, king of Judaea. He could hardly believe his luck. Of course the Parthians had not easily been removed from Judaea. It had taken three years before he had been enthroned in Jerusalem, carried in upon the blood-stained swords of Roman legionaries. But Rome was back to stay, and with her, was Herod. Much, though, still had to be done before happier times could be enjoyed.

The greatest problem for Herod was that, though he had officially embraced the Jewish faith, he was not a natural Jew, but an Idumean, an Edomite, a descendant of Israel's brother Esau. Jews were told not to despise Edomites, but these two 'brother-nations' had a long history of rivalry and, at times, enmity. Herod had never been really accepted by the Jews as their king. The fading Hasmonean dynasty, set aside by Rome, had proven to be a constant thorn in his side. Shortly before entering Jerusalem, he had married Mariamne granddaughter of the Hyrcanus his father had served under. But this alliance with the Hasmoneans, by which he hoped to strengthen his position, instead had brought trouble to his own family. Mariamne, but especially her violent and unscrupulous mother, Alexandra, had despised Herod's mother and sister, Salome, making the latter their implacable enemy. Salome played on Herod's insecurities and jealousy and over the next twelve years, one by one, the Hasmoneans had been destroyed.

By then, Herod's power base, Rome, had ended the violent upheavals of its Civil Wars. Only one man could now lead Rome and the rivals, Antony and Octavian had engaged in the final struggle. Herod had been a loyal supporter of Antony, 'Rome in the east'. But Antony had succumbed to the famed beauty and charms of the Egyptian queen Cleopatra and Cleopatra had desired to be queen of Jerusalem too. Herod's position had thus been threatened.

The battle between the giants had taken place at Actium twenty-seven years before. Antony and Cleopatra had both perished. Herod, who had assisted Antony with a force, had the immense good fortune to miss the battle; at the time he had been away on an expedition against the Arabs. Along with all the other kings of the east, he had run to congratulate Octavian, soon to take the title 'Augustus', on his victory.

Once again his father, Antipater's, policy had worked. Herod had said quite openly that he had loyally supported Antony, but that he would now do exactly the same for Augustus. Actium's victor assented and confirmed Herod as king. The old king shook his head in wonder; how fate had favoured him again. The threat from Cleopatra had been removed, and he not only held onto his throne but also became good friends with both Augustus and his very capable general, Agrippa. Augustus, with all rivals now eliminated, sailed into calmer more magnificent years. He was a great builder and it is said that he found Rome made of brick and left her made of marble. What he did for Rome, Herod attempted for Judaea.

The old king's mind turned to his own buildings. His construction projects fell neatly into three categories: Firstly Rome. Rome owned the Mediterranean, it was her sea. Judea at its eastern edge was most suitably approached by Rome from the water, but the country lacked any great natural harbour with which to welcome Roman traders...and warships. The solution had been the construction of the port of Caesarea Maritima with its theatre that ostentatiously looked out towards the Mediterranean...and to Rome. This port was the great anchor that held the province to the empire.

Secondly the Jews. As King of the Jews, Herod had begun a magnificent new temple in Jerusalem. The new building far outdid the scruffy little hovel that it replaced and, with its white stone and gold decorations, even outshone the original temple built by Solomon himself. As always, Herod had been very careful to observe Jewish religious sensitivities; only priests had been allowed to build the holy place. Yet Rome had to be honoured and her golden eagle had been placed on its gable. For the temple was also Rome's gracious gift to the Jewish people and her acknowledgement that the Jewish God held a special place in her admiration.

At least that is how Herod sometimes put it. Certainly, since Julius Caesar, Rome had allowed considerable freedom to its Jewish population to worship its 'god' as it chose. But what a strange 'god' those Jews worshipped. When Pompey had marched into Jerusalem sixty years before, annexing Judaea for Rome, he had himself entered the temple and its 'Holy of holies' and found...nothing. Such devotion to 'nothing' was basically incomprehensible to Rome, but, if the god wasn't there, the devotion was and had to be placated if it were not to rise in resistance to *the Pax Romana*. But resist it had, and recently too. Those hot-headed young fools, those pupils of Judas and Matthias, should have left the temple eagle well alone. The old king's jaw set in determination; he was right to have burned them. They had the new temple, why did they grasp for more.

Thirdly, there was Herod himself. This third category was less loudly proclaimed even if it was, shall we say, closer to his heart. The old king chuckled again. Among his several fortresses were two beautifully constructed, provisioned and garrisoned. One, Herodion, was built where he had fought against a detachment of Parthians when he had escaped from them years before. Atop its mound and within two hours of his palace in Jerusalem it marked his personal victory over Parthia...and was an ideal 'bolt-hole' in case of uproar in the city. The second was Masada, his refuge after that skirmish at Herodion. Down beside the Dead Sea, perched high on a table whose cliffs plunged to the valley floor, Masada was an impregnable fortress surrounded by desert and looking down on all who might approach. It would serve well should the Parthians invade again...or if the whole country rose in revolt. He could be incarcerated in it within hours there to comfortably await rescue by the legions of the eagle.

There was to be no risk to Herod's person!

This philosophy governed his diplomacy. Externally Rome must be honoured, vertically God was officially honoured, and internally Herod must be secure. For the person of Herod held the whole fabric together. Rome trusted him, God had blessed him and had permitted himself, Herod the Idumean, to build the new temple to His honour...and the Jews by and large tolerated the Edomite. Herod was the link that held Jerusalem and Rome together; he must be preserved.

Sadly this had meant that certain people who had risen up against his person had had to be dealt with. This was regrettable, especially when such people had been members of his own household, but entirely understandable. There was nothing personal; policy had demanded it. If Herod went, the whole house could easily fall and that indeed would be with a great crash.

The old king stared into the dancing flames of the fire kindled before him and brooded, a glass of wine gently rotating in his hands. It had been regrettable! He had loved Mariamne with great passion. Aristobulus, her younger brother, whom Herod had once hoped to serve under, had had to be drowned. Then the mutilated Hyrcanus, whom Herod had so ostentatiously welcomed back from Babylon, had to be removed on the charge of plotting with the Arabs. A year later, his beloved Mariamne fell from grace and had to be executed; shortly afterwards, her mother Alexandra went the same way. Recently, Mariamne's beautiful, popular....but Hasmonean sons, Alexander and Aristobulus had had to be strangled at Samaria. What had Augustus quipped? 'It is better to be Herod's pig than Herod's son'. For, as a 'good Jew' Herod would not kill a pig, but his own sons were another matter. Why couldn't they learn? Even now that imbecile Antipater, his eldest son, was imprisoned for exalting himself as the next king. What! Was Herod already dead? No! It would soon be Antipater that would be dead, the plans were already in motion and a new will had already been drafted.

The old king put the cup deliberately, firmly on the table. Herod must exalt, but as soon as he caught that glimmer of haughtiness in the exalted's eyes, Herod must debase. Why did they not realise that they had to stay low? It was not personality, but policy! Rome had set the Hasmoneans aside and a new dynasty, Herod's, was in the making. Out with the old and in with the new; it had always been thus. To leave elements of the old, invited intrigue and attacks on his person, therefore on Judaea's delicate relations with Rome. This was the one thought that brought the old king comfort and a measure of peace amid the afflictions of age and infirmity. For even now his body was shot through with pain in his lower parts. Wine, infused with myrrh, kept some of the pain at bay, but the confounded physicians had been all but useless and too much wine was rotting his kidneys. The old king moved uncomfortably on his padded couch; at times the agony brought moisture to his eyes. And now, on top of succession plans and severe pain...now there was this new item to deal with.

They had come from the east, from the old enemy Parthia. They were not spies that was clear, their demeanour and openness was child-like in the extreme. Indeed, it was this very naïveté that was so unnerving. The king had been used to outwitting schemers not baby-seekers. They had been so alarmingly simple; 'We have come looking for him who has been born King of the Jews'. As soon as the court heard these words there had been immediate shut-down. All eyes had been fixed upon the old king and his eyes suddenly...gave absolutely nothing away. It had indeed been a beautiful piece of acting. A look of simple surprise, a tone of joy in the question and he had met these (what were they?) magi on their own terms. The court took their cue and knew precisely what to do. No fear was even hinted at, no alarm and certainly no tittering at the king's supreme bit of drama.

The old king had expressed a certain ignorance and had asked the magi to wait in the atrium until he could supply them with the information they needed. They were carefully entertained there whilst Herod consulted with his theologians. For Herod had immediately understood what many in his court had not, that these wise men had come to Jerusalem looking for that mythological great king of the Jews, the Messiah.

That mention of him should be made was not in itself unusual. There was a lot of talk about the coming of the Messiah, especially when the Roman boot pressed hard on the Jewish neck, but what these men were clearly saying was something new; that the Messiah had arrived. He was here. He had been born somewhere and it was vital for Herod to ascertain that place and the time. His chief priests and scribes supplied the first answer; some prophet had foretold, apparently, that Messiah would be born in Bethlehem. Herod was prepared to accept the wisdom (or was it credulity?) of his own wise men sufficiently to consider little Bethlehem the place; but what of the time? That crucial piece of information was one that Herod did not want others to share. For, immediately, almost as a reflex action, a clear and decisive response was etching itself into the old pretender's mind.

It was early evening before the three enquirers were granted another audience with the king. It was brief and to the point. It was also very personal. The court's daily business, he told them, had been completed and the courtiers had been dismissed. He himself was about to dine but had just now been reminded that they were still in the atrium waiting upon him. In this way he apologised for the privacy of their audience. He moved quickly on to say that he was able to supply an answer to their question. Although very busy, he had made time to enquire of his own wise men and there was, apparently, a piece of wisdom that they had either overlooked, or not encountered. The one born to be king of the Jews was to be born in a small town to the south, not far away, by the name of Bethlehem. However, there was a problem, for, although it was eagerly anticipated by all, there had, as yet, been no report of the king's birth. Perhaps it had not yet taken place then?

This last question prompted the discussion that Herod so eagerly sought. No, the magi were sure he had appeared by now, for they had seen his natal star some time ago. It had been simple for the king to ask innocuously, as a matter of mere interest, how long ago this star had appeared.
"About ten months since." Was the reply.
"That surprises me," Herod remarked mildly, "why then has it taken you so long to get here?"
Their accounts of pausing for certainty and further enquiry, of the need for permission to travel, of delays on the way etc. etc. was mere formality to

him. Herod had his second vital clue. But he still did not have the baby. The next move, he knew, would involve a gamble; he had to trust these men and to do that, he had to win their trust in him.

"As you know, the birth of the Messiah is eagerly awaited by many, myself included. Indeed, as one presently holding the title King of the Jews, I consider myself merely a steward of that position for it has long been my ambition to be the one to cast my own crown at his feet in worship. You may be aware of my own deep devotion to our God, indeed, I have been permitted to make my own modest contribution to preparations for Messiah's arrival. You may have noticed the new temple in Jerusalem? If indeed what you say is true, and, though we do occasionally meet with charlatans, I am prepared to believe you, then it is an event entirely worthy of the celestial body you mention. I therefore beg of you, do this frail elderly monarch a great service. Go yourselves to Bethlehem, and make a careful search for the child and should you find him, send word to me that I may approach my king in adoration even as you seek to do."

It had been a long speech, had it done the trick?

Something leaped within him as he sensed they had taken the bait. Their own child-like faith in their venture was prepared to welcome the appearance of such in others. Indeed, their own great sacrifices made in pursuit of the king had rendered them

141

particularly vulnerable to a deception cloaked with a mantle of warm interest and the semblance of a faith like their own. In that moment they had all the innocence of the dove and none of the guile of the serpent. Herod was sure they had grasped the glove without feeling the cold iron hand beneath it. He moved swiftly on to close the meeting. They must be shown sufficient sympathy to believe him but not an excess that would arouse their suspicions. It was all very business-like yet warmed with an interest that had, he felt sure, secured their trust in his good intentions. Herod had retired to his private rooms satisfied that his dramatic cloak had concealed the dagger. A few days from now they would return with news of the baby's precise whereabouts in Bethlehem; the rest would be simple.

But they did not return.

He gave them several days to make their enquiries, then began to make some of his own. The reports were not encouraging. According to his informants, the magi had not made any search in Bethlehem, in fact, no-one was sure that they had even entered the town. Three strangers had stayed in one of the inns the day after Herod had met with the magi. The descriptions seemed to match. But they had asked no questions, slept much of the day and left in the evening, but in what direction no-one knew.

This was confusing. It taxed the old king's mind for several days as he continued waiting. Surely the men could not have lost their way to Bethlehem. No reports of brigands came in; they had not been found dead on the road. Yet why were there no reports of questions being asked in Bethlehem? It was impossible to think that they had entered the town, immediately found the child, made their worship and had decided not to return to Herod.

Yet, gradually, over the next few days this was the only scenario that began to make sense. How had they so quickly found the child? Herod interrogated his wise men on the appearance of an unusual star recently, but again, there had been nothing. Perhaps they had simply given up and gone home without wishing to report their failure to the king. But that too was ridiculous; you don't travel that distance for weeks without securing the object of your pilgrimage. So they must have found the baby then! How, Herod neither knew nor cared. The growing apprehension that he had been outwitted by these child-like magi fuelled a formidable determination.

Plan 'B' would have to be executed.

So it was that, one evening, Herod had another private meeting with the two officers he trusted most. Not merely captains of hundreds, they were also used to rendering their king special service.

The ageing monarch exhibited considerable discomfort as he outlined the plan. Excruciating pain, shooting through his abdomen, made the giving of sound instructions extremely difficult at times. More than once he stopped until the agony subsided. But, at last, the plan was communicated in its entirety.

Some days before the event, Roman officials were to appear in Bethlehem to make the announcement that discrepancies had been discovered in the information given in the recent census. Rome apologised for this; the offenders had been punished, but it was necessary to re-take the census of Bethlehem and its surrounding villages. This was to be done on a certain day and, so as not to cause unnecessary disruption of the town's normal business, would be conducted in tents a short distance outside the city itself. As the people gathered at the tents on the day, they would be informed that the declarations would be done in groups. First the elderly, then those families with no children...and so on.

On the day, all went smoothly and according to plan. The elderly were registered first in order to cause them as little discomfort as possible, and dismissed. Then families with no children for they could be interviewed quickly and allowed back to their business. Those with older children were next so that they could return to their tasks.

Finally, all that were left were families from
Bethlehem and its surrounds with small children.

A pre-arranged signal was then sent to the two
officers. A minute later their cavalry detachments
that were passing nearby turned towards
Bethlehem. One sealed the census area from
Bethlehem to prevent interference from any mob
from the town. The second hundred surrounded
the families waiting by the tents, dismounted and
began their grim business. Any obstructing adult
was cut down. Small children that looked as though
they were two or under, were examined to separate
male and female and the males all run through. The
whole business, lasted less than five minutes and
left sixty-three babies and toddlers and several
parents dead around the tents. Interference from
the town was prevented and the whole troop,
together with census officials, rode off in the
direction of Jerusalem.

The wailing continued until voices were exhausted.

The old king had just sealed the death warrant for
his eldest son, Antipater, when the two officers
waited upon him with their report. The mission had
been completely successful; there was no reason to
think that any boy under two, within Bethlehem or
its locality remained alive. Herod dismissed the
officers with the promise of a handsome gift to

show his gratitude for their loyalty in what was a regrettable, but necessary, action. Once again they had done well to protect their monarch from his enemies. It mattered little to Herod that, two days later, one of those two officers took his own life by falling on his sword; what was necessary had been done. The old king winced in pain, but chuckled to himself. Once again fate had smiled on him; strange to think that the fortunate Edomite had even outwitted Israel's God.

Shortly thereafter, Antipater had been executed. Five days later, Herod himself died in excruciating pain. The Jewish elders who had been assembled at the Hippodrome to be slaughtered at his death so that Judaea might really weep at his passing...were spared.

The old king's body was entombed near Herodion three miles from Bethlehem, the site of his last great 'victory'.

7. The Father: Joseph (Part II)

The words of the old shepherd resounded through
Joseph's mind long after Matthew and the others
had returned to the hills; 'You be a father to him.'
Coming from the older man they were both a
comfort, and a challenge. What did it mean to be a
'father'? Of course any ordinary man could 'father' a
child, but to really be a father – what did that
involve? Joseph had his role models, pre-eminently
his own abba, but they had been fathers to ordinary
sons...not to a son like Jesus. He knew of the
occasional man who had had to bring up someone
else's son, the child of a dead relative, but he was in
a unique position with the responsibility of bringing
up the Son...of God. He felt wonderfully chosen, yet
entirely inadequate; Matthew's commission had
been a great encouragement.

Unable to move either mother or child, the father
had to stay put in foreign Bethlehem. His first task
was to get the family out of the cowshed. As soon as
he could leave Mary for a few hours at a time, he
took up odd jobs around the town, doing them for a
pittance. He was stuck and felt trapped. He was
desperate to earn, but, with no bargaining power,
he had to take what he could get. He consoled
himself that this would only be for a few weeks,
then he could move the family back to Nazareth.

Eight days after the birth, much of his hard earned cash went on hiring the surgeon to perform the baby's circumcision. As 'father' it was his duty to ensure this was done, but, as with others, he felt too insecure about performing it himself. It sounded strange when the surgeon pronounced his name, 'Jesus son of Joseph'. He felt an urge to try to explain why that wasn't precisely the case...but said nothing. He winced as the steel cut through the soft flesh and his own chest rose with the baby's as Jesus let out a scream of pain. 'Welcome to the Covenant with Abraham; welcome too to a world of pain. Joseph wanted so much to protect Jesus from that. The operation carved out an emotional bond between the two even as now Joseph found himself officially...the father.

Normally it was the case that a man would adopt a child, and indeed this is what Joseph felt he was doing, but he could not entirely escape the idea that it was he who was the one being adopted. 'Jesus' – the name given supernaturally and independently to both Mary and himself – 'Jehovah Saves'; there was no such name among any of his ancestors. Normally his firstborn would have been called Mattan after his own father, or Eleazer after his beloved grandfather. He had given the baby that name in obedience; it bound Jesus to him yet also the very name indicated a difference, a separation.

Five weeks later came the next ceremony; the
'dedication of the firstborn'. This recalled the last
and worst of the ten plagues on Egypt, the death of
the firstborn. God had paid for Israel's release from
slavery with the firstborn sons of Egypt. In doing so
He had a right to the firstborn sons of Israel. Israel
had to redeem those sons with a sacrifice. It meant
a trip to Jerusalem, there to make the sacrifice in the
temple. It was the family's first journey outside of
Bethlehem and for once Joseph was thankful for
David's town – it was a lot closer to the temple than
Nazareth was. It would not be too onerous a
burden on the mother and baby.

Again the mixed feelings rose up in Joseph. He was
dedicating his firstborn to God, yet it wasn't really
his firstborn was it? It was God's. Joseph found
himself dedicating God's firstborn to Him. At times
this was just confusing, but he was officially the
father now and the ceremony had to be done.

The arrangements in Jerusalem filled Joseph with
that shame he had felt in the cowshed. There, in the
temple precinct, the gold on the huge new building
glistening in the afternoon sunlight, Joseph's
extreme poverty was again open for all to see. He
could only afford the cheapest of sacrifices to
redeem 'his' son from God. Not a bull or a ram like
some others near him; this father handed over a few
small coins, received the two pigeons and stood,
head hung a little low, in line waiting for the priest

to make the required sacrifice on his behalf. Again, Joseph felt uncomfortable, embarrassed. Of course he would have wanted to make more of the event, but they had nothing 'more'; he could hardly lodge and feed the family as it was let alone pay for ceremonies. A wave of resentment swept over him as he stood in the line, but this time it was easier to emerge from it and Joseph had recovered in time to thank the Lord for the safe arrival of 'his' firstborn and to receive him back with gratitude from the One to whom he rightfully belonged.

Moments later, almost in answer to his worship, something very unusual happened.

Joseph, still slightly embarrassed, had moved a little way from the main crowd and had rejoined Mary in the Court of the Women. He didn't notice the old man at first. It was Mary who caught sight of him starring at them. She motioned to Joseph as he began to approach them. They moved away but he followed. As the old man drew near, the father sensed that same defensive attitude rising within him as he had felt when the shepherds had come to the stable. What did he want? He was looking intently at the bundle in Mary's arms and seemed almost in a dream. Joseph stood between him and his son.

'May I?' Suddenly the ancient seemed to see the parents as he took the father's arm. Joseph looked at Mary for her response and was a little unnerved when she transferred the bundle into his arms. Something strange was happening; they didn't know this man at all, yet she was entrusting Jesus into his care; Joseph was bewildered and still on the defensive, ready to catch the bundle should it accidentally fall...or worse.

As the ancient held the new-born, something began to happen. A bond seemed to flood out of the old towards the new. A smile spread over the old man's wrinkled countenance, yet tears dropped from his eyes onto the wrappings. Joseph looked bemused; what was going on? Moments later the ancient lifted the bundle slightly and looked to heaven. To others standing around it probably appeared to be the proud grandfather giving thanks, but this was no ordinary act of gratitude. Simeon's prayer had a finality about it. It was the prayer of one about to pass on, of one whose life's purpose had been fulfilled – right at the end. From the old man's words Joseph understood that the Holy Spirit, the real father of the boy, had revealed to this man that he would not die before he had seen the Lord's Christ. He had been holding God to this promise for decades; years before Mary, even Joseph had been born. This was incredible! Joseph just stood back and marvelled. It was indeed a bit like the shepherds all over again.

Moments after that, something else amazing
happened.

Hardly had Simeon returned Jesus to Mary's arms
than another ancient approached. She knew
Simeon and obviously knew something of the
promise to him, for she too began to give thanks for
the baby. Joseph caught the look of amazement in
Mary's eyes – he must have had that same look in
his own moments before. The old lady, Anna by
name, was, like Simeon, looking forward to Israel's
redemption at the hands of the Messiah. She was
open about a personal tragedy that had struck
when, after only seven years of marriage, her
husband had died. Now eighty-four, she had
devoted the rest of her life to God, remaining in the
temple constantly in prayer, in fasting and...in
expectation. She was convinced that the new
temple building was a sign that Messiah would soon
come. Indeed she knew Simeon and his word; his
faith fuelled her own expectation...and prayers. As
the young couple stood and stared at the old, an
eternal bond seemed to wrap around them. Mary
and Joseph, the physical and official parents looked
into the eyes of Simeon and Anna, the long-patient
parents of faith and prayer. Anna, like any proud
grandmother, was soon telling close confidents the
good news of the birth.

But one thing from this encounter bothered Joseph.

After he had thanked God, Simeon had blessed them and then spoken to them - well to Mary really. And Joseph could not forget his words. 'This child is destined to cause the falling and rising of many in Israel...and a sword will pierce your own soul too.' This had been rather disturbing. Joseph tried to think it all through but found he could only get so far. They, the shepherds and now Simeon all believed Jesus to be the Messiah. Yet he, indeed Israel generally, was expecting the Messiah to come out of heaven as a mighty warrior, vanquishing Israel's enemies, judging the nation (Now there could be the 'falling and rising of many in Israel!) and ruling over the nations in the place of David. How, therefore, did this picture fit with the defenceless bundle at Mary's breast? And what of this 'sword' that would pierce Mary's soul? Joseph felt worried by this; he wanted to know, to protect. What grief would come to Mary? And, why would it be to her and not to him? The father was confused by it all and - not a little apprehensive. But he chose not dwell on it; another few weeks and mother and child would be strong enough to return to Nazareth.

But that was not to be!

It was a few days later that it happened. The family was bedded down in the draughty hovel that was all they could afford, when Joseph was awakened by a feint tapping at the door. He dismissed it at first – the wind or something. But as it continued he gradually came round to the awareness that somebody was outside. Who could it be? They hardly knew anyone in the town, certainly no-one who'd have any business with them at this time of night...unless...unless it was those shepherds again – but no, that business had been closed and veiled in strange secrecy. As he got up and moved to the door, the father remembered having seen old Matthew once, in the street, but the old man merely gave a knowing look and went his way. Who then could it be?

Joseph carefully opened the door, his foot planted firmly behind it, and peered out into the darkness. Actually, a strange quiet light seemed to fill the street and lit up three men outside; one at the door and two still up on their camels. What was this? A strange accent yet brought fluent Greek to his ears. "We seek the king. He is here, yes?"
Joseph just stared for a moment. It was that same sensation he had had when the shepherds had spoken out of the night asking for a baby.
"We seek the king, the King of the Jews. He is here, yes?" The strange accent repeated itself softly out of the darkness.
"Uh...yes....he's here...but...eh...how...?" Joseph listened to himself still stumbling over his own reticence to believe what he knew to be true.
"May we please enter?"
Once again the father was about to say 'No!' but instead said 'Oh...yes.' and this time without Mary's

prompting. She was awake of course and now stood behind her husband, a murmuring Jesus in her arms.

"What is it Joseph?" Her sleepy voice made him turn around.

"Some men. They are seeking the King of the Jews."

"Well, shall we let them see him then?" Mary's matter-of-fact tone almost made him laugh. Why...couldn't...he...just...accept it all? The three strangers soon stood in the light of three small lamps looking at the baby. It was just like the shepherds all over again. Except...except that these were no shepherds and certainly not local.

For the three men began to remove their worn travelling cloaks to display richly ornamented garments concealed beneath. The father watched as, one by one, knelt for long minutes in prayer and worship...and not a few tears. Awe and reverence filled the little hut as each bowed in adoration at the rough crib Joseph had knocked together from some old planks he had found. Then, from among their travel bags they took out caskets and a vial...gifts.

The lid of the first box was opened and the father's eyes widened as pieces of gold gleamed warmly in the lamp-light. The lid of the second casket was removed to fill the hovel with a heady perfume...frankincense. The final gift, the vial, was presented. When the top was removed and Joseph caught its aroma it was one he knew well - the odour of medicine, of worship, of cosmetic and...of death. Joseph was instantly reminded of the scent that accompanied the rituals surrounding the passing of his grandfather and parents....liquid myrrh. Once again, the father stood in bewilderment. He wanted to know what all this meant and began to question the men.

The couple listened in amazement once again as the account these strangers had to tell unfolded in their hearing. They had come from the east, from way beyond Babylon and had been travelling for weeks. They were magi, of the eastern schools of wise men. They had seen a star. The star had alerted them to the birth of the King, but then had vanished. They had gone to Jerusalem to find him, but had been told that he was to be born here in Bethlehem. Just that evening, they had been speaking with the old king, Herod, who had encouraged them in their quest. Just after they had left the palace, discussing how they could approach their search for the child, to their amazement, the star they had seen months before suddenly reappeared and had 'led' them to this house. Out of sheer curiosity Joseph went outside, but came back shaking his head; he could see no 'star', what was that all about? He asked them further about their worship and the gifts they had brought with them.

As the magi explained their gifts Joseph's mind whirled with implications. The child was the King of the Jews, he was also a great High Priest and...he was a sacrifice. His brows furrowed and his head shook as he began to wrestle with his responses. How was he, a carpenter, supposed to train up a king? He was, yes, a son of David, but that was a far distant association that had no connections with his everyday life...well, until recently that is. Also, how could he in any sense prepare Jesus for a supreme act of sacrifice...the ceremony of circumcision had unnerved him enough. His heart now went out to Jesus, he wanted to protect his son, to give to him, to watch him grow and to delight in his progress...not sacrifice him! And what of a priest? Joseph sought to live a righteous life, to obey God's laws through Moses, he always had...but to train another to the holiness of the priesthood – that was quite another matter. Priests were from the tribe of Levi, not Judah. How was a humble carpenter to educate a high priest?

The three magi took their leave. The gifts had been hidden carefully away. But now, as Mary slept peacefully beside him, an old worry engulfed the father again and left him starring into the darkness, pondering.

The shepherds, Simeon, and now these magi...they all confirmed again what Joseph knew – that Jesus was conceived by the Holy Spirit. Mary's womb had become a holy place. For Joseph there was a growing apprehension that he had no right of 'entry' to that place. The fear that occasionally assailed him, came back with renewed force; perhaps they ought to abstain from normal marital relations. Perhaps Jesus' conception now demanded a sacrifice from him, one that he really did not want to make. As he turned these things over in his mind, thankfully, two things challenged this fear and in the end brought him peace and hope. One that other, ancient, births had had miraculous aspects – Rachel, Hannah and pre-eminently Sarah. Recently too there had been the amazing birth of a son to Mary's aged cousin Elizabeth. God had intervened it was clear, but both Rachel and Hannah at least had gone on to have other children. God's miracle had not put a stop to normality. Secondly the angel had told Joseph not to be afraid to take Mary as his wife. He was to be to her a husband, with all that that would normally entail. The fourth watch of the night had started before the father fell asleep.

Then, it was just two nights later that Joseph himself had a second dream.

Again there was that exquisite visionary encounter with an angel. This time, however, the words were much less comforting. 'Get up, take the child and his mother and flee to Egypt. Remain there until I tell you, for Herod is about to search for the child to destroy him.' Joseph's response was immediate and uncompromising. That slight apprehension he had felt when the magi spoke of their meeting with Herod, was now pressed upon him with violent confirmation; all their lives were in urgent, mortal danger. Waves of panic swept over him as he fumbled with the lamp, packed their few belongings, carefully concealed the precious gifts among the supply of linens and kitchen items and saddled the donkey. Weeks before, they had entered Bethlehem as the stars had begun to show, now they padded quietly down the main street at dead of night.

'Halt! Who are you and what's your business at this hour?'
Joseph's heart thumped as the night watchmen apprehended them.
'Joseph, a son of David (That might help he thought, but his mind raced desperately for a reason) uh, we...have just this hour received bad news of my mother and are leaving immediately to tend her.'
'I've heard no-one about, what are you carrying?'
'Our few belongings, the bundle there is our new-born son.' Joseph was terrified that a search would reveal the gifts...precious items he would never be able to explain.
Mary pulled back the loose covering to reveal Jesus tiny face. The watchmen seemed satisfied; 'He's a young 'un for a night journey isn't he?'
'Uh...yes...but we don't have far to go.' (That wasn't quite true either!)
'Well, be on your way then.'

With huge relief Joseph left the town and turned onto the road that would take them to Gaza and then on to Egypt. As the fire of dawn began to appear in the eastern sky, they found a grove of trees and slept. Mid-morning, though, and they were on their way again, with Joseph keen to put miles between them and Jerusalem as quickly as possible. There were not many on the desert road that day so the appearance of a cloud of dust behind them convulsed Joseph with an apprehension that only intensified as occasional flashes of sunlight glinted off lance heads. The couple moved to the side of the road as the detachment of cavalry approached.

Joseph put his hand into Mary's and felt the tremors that mirrored his own. There was no place to hide in this deserted area, they were a solitary couple with a baby boy clearly moving away from Judaea and these, he could now see, were Roman cavalry, soldiers answerable to Herod. The couple attempted to hide their terror as the unit trotted up to the place where they stood. 'Lord save us!' Joseph breathed, his heart pounding. The small troop examined them, but then continued down the road.

The couple hesitantly moved back out into the road after the riders. They saw them later, in Gaza; the detachment was a relief for the post there. Joseph stayed in the town long enough only to buy provisions and wait for a caravan to assemble to take them across the desert dunes to Egypt. Once there he made for the large Jewish population of Alexandria to find refuge in the anonymity of the city crowds. In the bazaar they could do another thing; sell some of the costly gifts to enable them to rent lodgings and eat whilst they waited for their next instructions.

Given the frequent movement that occurred between Judaea and Alexandria, it was relatively simple to keep up with news from home. Sometime after their arrival in Egypt, it transpired that Herod's reign was over, though not before the expected next ruler, Antipater, had been executed. Rumours also circulated of an atrocity in the small town of Bethlehem. Joseph urgently wanted to know more, but hesitated to draw undue attention to himself. He used the excuse that it was his ancestral home to find out further details.

The horror, it was said, mainly involved children and then seemed to be aimed at males. Some were saying that the king was mad, that his mind had been deranged. Hadn't he killed his eldest son just days before his own death? A minority, however, were linking it with the appearance of some strangers at Herod's court several days before who had asked after Messiah's birth. Despite Herod's insistence that it should not do so, this news had quickly leaked out causing much apprehension in Jerusalem. Joseph was immediately convinced that the minority position was the correct one. What had appeared at the time to be a journey that could endanger mother and child had actually saved all their lives. The celestial vision had been right again - and again, Joseph was right to have obeyed. When, some nights later, he had a third dream in which the angel of the Lord told him to take the child and his mother back to Israel, his obedience was instinctive and they soon joined another caravan eastwards towards Gaza.

By the time they reached that town however, Joseph was plagued with doubts. Surely they could not return to Bethlehem still raw in the agony of its grief. He was equally uncertain about Jerusalem. They were known there too. Both Simeon and the aged Anna had identified Jesus as the Messiah; they would only have to let one word out for child to be cut in two. In Gaza the news reached them that Herod's son, Archelaus, was now ruler in Judaea. This did it for Joseph; he knew some of the rumours about this man's offences, arrogance and repression; the father was determined that they should not make for the capital. The angel had said go into 'the Land of Israel', but, where in that land would be safe for them? They paused for several days in Gaza whilst Joseph thought...and prayed.

As he did so, other news came in. Herod had, apparently, willed that his kingdom be divided between his three sons, Archelaus, Antipas and Philip, and Galilee had been given to Antipas. The little Joseph knew about this man still made him hesitant to return there however. A fourth dream, warning him against Judaea, ended his hours of prayer. It must be Nazareth...unless another dream intervened. For by now Joseph felt confident that God's hand was upon them and that they would be both guided and protected. If his home town was not the right place, surely the Lord would say so. In the event, He did not.

So it was that Joseph and Mary finally returned home to a warm welcome from concerned friends and family who immediately began to dote upon the baby. As Mary settled down to her new role as a mother in her community, Joseph returned to his workshop, took the crib off of his bench, gave it to a very grateful wife and began again to put his shoulder to the work he knew so well.

Joseph gladly resumed some possession of his life...and his wife, for with the return to normality, the couple began the new adventure of marital relations that soon issued in other children. Just as Hannah, after the special birth of Samuel, had five other children, so now Mary was to have another six; the four boys, James, Joses, Simeon and Judah and two girls. The distractions of such a household soon softened and dampened the hard and deeply etched memories surrounding the birth of Jesus. Yet there were numerous occasions when Joseph looked at Jesus upon Mary's knee, or at play with the other children or grappling with his father's tools in the workshop, and the father would stop for a moment and remember and ponder that time when he had been wrenched from his life of quiet normality and cast onto the highway of stress, uncertainty and mortal danger.

Joseph remained in Nazareth. He never went back to Bethlehem, never returned to Egypt and never had another significant dream. Instead he became a model father in Nazareth, bringing up his seven children in the instruction of the Torah and the fear of the Lord. Life fitted back into the shape it always should have been and the memories continued to soften and fade.

Then, all at once, with a terrific jolt, Joseph found himself in the middle of a final trauma and one that taxed his faith to the limit again.

As usual, Joseph had taken Mary and the children to Jerusalem for the Passover. By now, all fears of the capital were well behind him. Two years before, Archelaus had been removed from power and a Roman prefect governed the city. This, combined with the anonymity of the festive crowds, meant that Joseph's mind was far more concerned with the safety of their little ones than with any worries about Jesus who by now was almost a man anyway.

The festival had gone well and the family, together with others from Nazareth, began to make their way back home. As usual, the three older boys had gone off in different directions and were with the families of their friends, just as two of two of Simeon's friends walked along with them. It was only in the evening, as families ate together, that the tangle of children would sort itself out. So it was that James and Joses returned to them as the caravan stopped to camp for the night. Unusually though, Jesus did not appear for his meal. Never mind, perhaps he had been invited by others. The real panic began when he did not re-join the family to sleep. James and Joses were sent among the other families to bring him in but returned minutes later saying they could not find him anywhere. Joseph did not need Mary's alarm to spur him to action, but it did feed into his own. Both parents left their children with close friends and began an increasingly frantic search among the festive throng, but to no avail; Jesus was nowhere to be found.

Joseph hardly slept at all that night. He knew they must return to Jerusalem. Together with an older couple from Nazareth who had volunteered to return with them to look after the children, they hurried back to reach the city at about the ninth hour. Their Jerusalem campsite, though, was all but deserted and the handful of families still there had no news. Joseph now looked towards the towering walls; they would have to scour the city for their lost son.

As they searched the streets, asking at shops, inns and in the market place, a growing horror enveloped the couple, one that neither was able to voice. They had been entrusted with God's special child, but their careless neglect now had put his life at risk. Late that evening, they returned to their family exhausted and dejected.

The next day was worse. Friends, acquaintances, strangers all were interrogated as were the city watch and magistrates, but no lost boy had been reported. Every failure to find Jesus deepened the dark, rocky valley of fear, regret and self-blame. They reminded themselves of Jesus' birth and the miracles that had accompanied it. They had not been perfect then either, yet the Lord had brought them through. Had they missed something in the return to normality in Nazareth? Had they neglected something they should have attended to? It could not be so! Surely the Lord would have spoken if they should have done something different, taken a new direction in life. Never, since Jesus' birth, had they prayed so much. They returned late to their family that second evening almost consumed with fear, clutching at a dwindling hope.

Spurred on by the battle within them between faith and sheer panic, they set out early the next morning. Now, with the festive throng gone, Jerusalem was returning to normality and a sense of post-celebration depression brooded over the city. Tired traders, resentful rubbish removers were all questioned. The couple went through every quarter of the city; some made them shudder, dearly wishing that Jesus were not there.

Finally, that afternoon, their search took them to the temple area itself. Certain places would be out of bounds to Jesus, as they were to them. Mary searched the Court of the Women, and Joseph the Court of the Israelite men, but without success. It was when they had re-joined one another and had begun to work round the colonnades that they sighted him. When they did so it was in probably the last place they would have expected him to be. Yet, there he was, as clear as day, in a colonnaded area where the teachers of the law were wont to gather and debate. Joseph grasped Mary's arm and pointed. For a moment they both just stood there and stared, waves of relief washing over their distressed souls. For there was Jesus, sitting in the midst of this distinguished group of scholars, listening and asking questions. Joseph watched mesmerised as learned eye-brows were raised and legal foreheads furrowed as doctors searched their own minds for apt replies to the boy.

At last though, with a shake of the head, Joseph respectfully approached the group. Mary was a little less respectful; her eyes were upon Jesus, and it was she who spoke first letting out her sheer frustration with the boy, 'Child, why have you done this to us? Can't you see that your father and I are out of our minds with worry, looking all over for you?' Joseph, apologising to the distinguished gathering, did not quite catch Jesus' response at that moment. They quickly removed him and, with much relief and great rejoicing, returned to their family and to Nazareth.

It was about a week later that Joseph, smiling, asked his wife why she looked so pensive at that moment. He never forgot the look in her eyes or her reply. "You remember Joseph, when we found Jesus in the temple? Did you hear what he said to me?" "No. Come to think of it, I don't." he said. "I was a bit overawed by the company he was keeping at the time." Joseph continued with a smile. "His first words really galled me Joseph, he said, 'Why did you need to look for me?' Why indeed! Husband, I tell you, after what we had been through, it was all I could do not to scream at the boy in that moment. But then he gave a reason and I cannot get it out of my mind. He said, 'Didn't you know I would have to be in my Father's house?'" "My Father's house." Joseph repeated. "What did he mean by that?"

Mary replied with a question, "Where did we find
him Joseph?"

"In the temple of course." But then the potential
significance of that began to dawn upon him. "In the
house of God", he murmured, almost in a dream.
"His father's house! Mary, do you suppose that
somehow...Jesus knows?"

"Joseph, I am sure of it. I have not told him, have
you?"

"Not a word."

"Then how does he know?"

"Well...uh..." Joseph was still wrestling with the
revelation; an explanation of it seemed beyond him
in that moment. Finally he blurted out, "I suppose
that since the Lord spoke to both you and I Mary...is
it not possible that He has also spoken to Jesus?"

"I can't help but think so Joseph, and yet, he's still
only a boy; you haven't yet released him to God in
his Bar Mitzvah."

"No, I haven't Mary. But then...perhaps...he was
never fully mine to release anyway."

Mary searched Joseph's face. He looked away,
wanting to reflect upon the words that had just
tumbled from his mouth. Memories of angelic
visitation, of Bethlehem, the shepherds, the magi
and of the flight to Egypt were shared in the silence.
All came flooding back as they tried to fix in place
this latest piece of the puzzle.

He knew! How were they to deal with this new
found sense of identity in Jesus? What would it

entail? It had already brought high tension, would it also cause disturbance, even destruction in the family?

They need not have worried for Jesus remained obedient to them.

'Never fully mine'. Joseph pondered his own words. His six other children were the pride of his life, but Jesus was unique and experience of his first son had taught him so much. Again he felt that wave of immense inadequacy as he struggled to rear the Son of God - even to this moment and nearly losing him in Jerusalem. But God had brought him safely through.

What did being a real father involve? For him, in those months surrounding Jesus' birth, it had felt as though a cart had been driven through his life; so much had changed, so much was different. Yet, as he had cried out to God, he had been answered in remarkable ways, and God had used him not only to do what needed to be done for the boy, but also to be the means to save his life. Joseph had come to know God's father-like care in far greater measure because of Jesus. Now, it seemed, Jesus knew God as Father for himself. Should Joseph worry or should he rejoice at this? Surely that was the greatest thing a father could do for his son wasn't it...to guide him towards his own relationship with God?

Joseph thought of the old shepherd's words again, 'You be a father to him'. They had been a call to faith; a call to believe what God had said to him that first time through the angel, to believe that it was possible. The carpenter mused: 'I could only love my son as I knew God's love for me. Only as I knew God's care for me, was I really able to begin to care for Jesus. I could only start to be a genuine father as I began to know the reality of God's fathering of me.'

Final Note

Dear Reader,

Well perhaps that was how it might have been.

Much, of course, is speculation, though I have attempted to remain as close to the biblical accounts as possible.

These stories began as an attempt to provide new insight for my family who were well accustomed to the Christmas accounts. The idea was that each year a new story would be read to my wife and children to stimulate reflection and renew interest. It is with their encouragement that I offer this book for publication.

If, by reading it, your understanding and appreciation of that first Christmas has in any way been enriched by these stories, then I shall be glad.

As John put it:

"We write this to make our joy complete."
(1 John 1.4)

Many thanks for your interest,

Chris.

By the same author:

Available now:

'Life Talks' Series: *Easter*
                       Pentecost

Board Games   *Where Jesus Walked*
                       Days of Daniel

Hopefully coming soon

Commentary on Matthew's Gospel

Musicals   *Born*   (A Christmas Musical)
                       Resurrected   (An Easter Musical)

Made in the USA
Charleston, SC
08 November 2015